LIL' MUFFIN DROPS THE MIC

ROMESH RANGANATHAN

ILLUSTRATED BY JAMES LANCETT

PUFFIN

PUFFIN BOOKS

UK | USA | Canada | Ireland | Australia
India | New Zealand | South Africa

Puffin Books is part of the Penguin Random House group of companies
whose addresses can be found at global.penguinrandomhouse.com

www.penguin.co.uk
www.puffin.co.uk
www.ladybird.co.uk

Penguin
Random House
UK

First published 2023
001

Set in 13.5/21.5 Macklin Text by Nigel Baines

Printed in Great Britain by Clays Ltd, Elcograf S.p.A.

The authorized representative in the EEA is Penguin Random House Ireland,
Morrison Chambers, 32 Nassau Street, Dublin D02 YH68

A CIP catalogue record for this book is available from the British Library

ISBN 978-0-241-64764-6

All correspondence to:
Puffin Books
Penguin Random House Children's
One Embassy Gardens,
8 Viaduct Gardens,
London SW11 7BW

Penguin Random House is committed to a
sustainable future for our business, our readers
and our planet. This book is made from Forest
Stewardship Council® certified paper.

people exercising in tracksuits that are too small for them, and there's less cake about when you go to visit people because they're all trying to eat healthily at this time of year. James thought that was ridiculous. Why on earth would you want to live your life without cake? It made no sense.

James's thoughts on baked treats were interrupted by a man coming towards him. The man wasn't looking where he was going because he was absolutely smashing through an enormous box of muffins, eating them so fast you'd think he'd just been told eating muffins was going to be made illegal in ten minutes. He was *loving* those cakes. Chunks and crumbs were flying all over the place. In fact, the man's face was covered in so much muffin debris that you couldn't be completely sure where his face ended and muffin began. What an animal!

James didn't say any of this out loud, of course. He just thought it as the man walked past. He definitely didn't have a problem with someone loving muffins – of course not. Muffins are incredible, particularly the triple-chocolate ones that

Lil' Muffin DROPS THE MIC

This book is dedicated to my wife and children, who had to deal with a long flight home with me asking them repeatedly if the story was any good.

have those little fudge chunks rammed in the top. James would sometimes buy a box of four, remove the fudge from three of them and put it all on the last one, creating a **SUPER MUFFIN**. He would then offer the other three to friends, saving the best muffin for himself. Although one time he dropped the super muffin on the floor in front of everyone. He pretended not to care, because people were watching, but if he'd been on his own he would have just picked up the muffin and eaten it anyway – that amount of fudge is worth catching floor disease for.

As the muffin man walked past James, he was eating so crazily that one of the muffins, possibly blueberry, fell from the huge box he was carrying. James watched it tumble to the ground, while also noting that the man was completely unaware that he had a muffin overboard. Imagine having so many that you don't even notice that you've lost one? What a glorious life this man must lead.

James was about to run after the man to tell him when he saw that the muffin hadn't stopped moving. It was rolling around in a way that you'd have to say was unusual. It's very rare to see a muffin on the move. Think about it. Have you ever seen one? Well, this muffin kept going. It rolled round and round faster and faster. Then it trundled towards James.

Ordinarily, this wouldn't have worried him; he'd have been happy to see a delicious muffin rolling his way. But this muffin seemed to be getting bigger. Yes, it was definitely growing. In fact, it was getting **bigger** so quickly that, as it moved towards James, he instinctively backed away. The muffin began to speed up, and it got larger and larger and larger. Soon it was moving so quickly that walking backwards wasn't going to cut it any more.

James was beginning to panic. He turned his back on the muffin, something he never thought he'd find himself doing, and ran. When he looked over his shoulder, the muffin was the size of a dog. He speeded up. He glanced behind him again. Now the muffin was the size of a car. He speeded up. He looked back once more, and the muffin was the size

of an even bigger car. James ran faster. He turned round, and the muffin was the size of a massive car! Turns out it's actually quite difficult to do size comparisons when you're trying to escape from a **MEGA MUFFIN**.

James was getting out of breath now, which

was a problem because the muffin didn't seem to be having the same issue. He couldn't go on much longer. He needed to evade the muffin somehow. But how? After a moment's pause, he decided his best bet would be to dive out of the way and perform a roll of his own. Then – hopefully – he'd be able to watch the beast muffin speed harmlessly by. He took a deep breath – it was now or never – and leaped on to the grass to the right of him and rolled for dear life.

As he came to a stop, James looked around dizzily to see where the muffin had ended up. But he couldn't spot it. Where was it? Oh well, it didn't matter – he'd escaped. Breathing a sigh of relief, James got up, dusted himself off, and was about to carry on walking when he heard a low rumbling. It sounded a bit like an earthquake.

AND THEN HE SAW IT.

The muffin was heading straight towards him again.

'Help! It's after me!' he shouted, sprinting away.

The muffin was too quick, though. Before he

knew it, it had caught him up, knocked him down and rolled right over his legs.

James wriggled, and then squirmed, and then wriggled some more. But he was trapped. He wondered if he might have to accept that he now lived under a **MEGA MUFFIN**. He would definitely be late for school now.

Just then, he noticed the muffin man running towards him. He was shouting something, but James couldn't hear what it was. It sounded like: 'You need a poo!' No, that couldn't be right. James strained to make out the words. Eventually, he was able to understand. The man was shouting: 'You have to get to school!'

'I know that!' James replied. 'But I'm trapped under this muffin!'

'Why are you talking about a muffin? You need to get up!' said the man.

'I will if you'll help me move it,' James said, frustrated. Surely it was perfectly obvious why he couldn't get up. He was pinned beneath a giant muffin!

'James, get up!'

Wait, why did the muffin man sound like James's mum?

'I AM STUCK UNDER A MUFFIN!' he bellowed.

James woke with a start. He wasn't trapped under a muffin; he was in bed. His mum was standing in front of him in her BoomBox dressing gown, holding a mug of coffee. BoomBox was her favourite boy band from when she was a teenager, and she'd never stopped loving them.

'Come on, Muffin Boy, get your bum out of bed!' his mum said before taking an enormous glug of coffee. 'I'm going to need another three cups of this before I leave the house.'

James looked down at his legs to see his rabbit, Graham, sound asleep. It seems weird to suggest that a rabbit could trap anyone's legs, but then Graham was no ordinary rabbit.

Brukka was sitting in the recording studio in his underpants. On the wall behind him in the vocal booth was a framed magazine cover of him not in his underpants, above the headline:

IS BRUKKA THE BIGGEST RAPPER IN THE WORLD?

In fact, all the walls in the studio were covered with gold and platinum discs from Brukka's previous albums. On the table in front of him was a half-eaten packet of Chocolate Digestives, and there were crumbs everywhere.

Brukka had just asked the producer to stop the beat, and in that moment they heard a voice shouting down the corridor. It was Brukka's manager, DP. Brukka could see him through the studio windows. He was wearing, as he always did, a brightly coloured suit that was slightly too big for him, trainers that didn't really go with the suit, and a pair of huge yellow sunglasses, and he was flailing his arms about. Brukka couldn't hear what he was saying, but DP looked annoyed. At one point, DP went to kick a bin in anger, but because his sunglasses were obscuring his vision he missed.

Brukka laughed to himself. *Why was DP always so dramatic?!*

'OK,' said Brukka. 'Let's play the beat again.'

The producer nodded and flicked a button. The deep bass intro to the track started, and Brukka began to nod his head as the beat arrived via his headphones. He saw DP walk into the room as he started to rap:

'Coming up against Brukka, man,
    you don't wanna risk it.
Rappers get crumbled like as if
    they was a biscuit.
Brukka starts rapping, and people
    feel festive.
Dip into my tea like I was a
    Digestive.
I have money, you can call me
    Rich Tea.
I'm well known like Hobnobs.
    You're not like Garibaldi –'

Brukka stopped and shook his head.

'This is **rubbish**, man!' he cried to the producer and DP. Why was he struggling to come up with good raps these days? He felt so uninspired – rapping about whatever was in front of him instead of things he really cared about.

DP clicked the button to talk to him in the booth.

'Is there a reason why you're doing this in your underpants, mate?' he asked.

'My tracksuit is too noisy. Every time I move, the mic picks up a rustling noise.'

DP started typing on his phone. 'I'm making a note to order some quieter tracksuits,' he said in a businesslike tone. He paused. 'I wonder if being in your underpants is what's making you think the song is bad?'

'What are you talking about?' Brukka asked.

'Well, I don't know – maybe you don't feel like a rapper. You look like you're about to go swimming, to be honest.'

'That's not the problem,' Brukka said grumpily.

'Even if I had *all* my clothes on, I'd still be doing a rubbish song about biscuits, man. Why am I talking about *biscuits*?'

'People like 'em, mate!' said DP soothingly. **'WHO DOESN'T LIKE BISCUITS?!'**

But Brukka had had enough. 'Nah, DP, it's not working today. The session's over, bro.' And with that he took his headphones off and left the booth. He walked into the room where DP and the producer were. They stared at him.

'What are you gawping at?' he asked.

'Erm, you're still in your underpants?' replied DP.

'Oh right, yeah,' Brukka mumbled, and went back into the booth to retrieve his tracksuit.

DP shook his head so much his sunglasses fell off.

James glanced at his phone. There was a message from his best friend Sara that said:

Yes! How could he have forgotten about the bake sale? It was the most important day of his secondary-school life so far, and probably, James realized, why he'd been having an anxiety dream about a giant muffin crushing him.

His legs were still feeling a bit numb from Graham lying on them, but the feeling slowly returned as he stumbled around his bedroom, trying to find his school uniform. Graham looked completely unbothered and absolutely massive as usual. He was bigger than any rabbit James had ever seen, or, in fact, any rabbit they could find on the internet.

A few years ago, before James's dad had left, James had begged and begged for a dog.

'We can't get a dog – it's way too much work!' his dad had said. But every day, when his dad got home from work, James would present him with articles and information about how to look after a dog, how to make it easy, how to do it without spending too much money.

James's mum could see how much he wanted

one, and eventually she'd softened. 'I'll look after it,' she said. 'But, James, you'll obviously have to help me. I am not dealing with all those poos on my own.'

'I don't mind helping out with that – I love poo!' James said excitedly, before realizing that this was actually a really weird thing to say.

'OK, fine, I'll look into it!' James's dad had said finally.

James was delighted. He gave his dad a list of his favourite breeds that he'd been researching, but also said that he really didn't mind. He just wanted a dog. He talked about nothing but dogs. Constantly telling anyone and everyone about the dog he was going to get.

Two days later, his dad came home with a large white cardboard box, the kind you might expect to find a cake in. James couldn't believe it. His dad had done it! James was about to be a dog owner! Unless this was a cake, of course.

'If this is a cake that looks like a dog, it's not funny,' he said. 'But if it's chocolate, I'll probably still eat it.'

They all sat down on the sofa, and James's dad handed him the box. It felt very animally, if that makes sense. James thought that when he saw the dog he might scream with joy, and then the dog would be terrified of him forever. He placed his face really close to the lid, so that the dog would see him first, reducing the chance it might prefer his parents. He opened the lid slowly and was greeted with the sight of a puppy that looked a hell of a lot like . . .

... **A TINY RABBIT**.

James looked at the rabbit, and then turned to his dad in utter confusion. His dad knew he wanted a dog – James couldn't have been clearer about that.

'Er, Dad, you do know that this isn't a dog, don't you? This is actually a rabbit.'

His dad laughed. 'Yes, of course I know that, James! This rabbit provides all the good, fluffy, cuddly stuff you get with a dog, but is a lot less hassle. You don't have to walk him, for a start. And the poos are much easier to deal with!'

James was pretty upset. How on earth had his dad thought a rabbit would be a good replacement for a dog? He'd had all these plans – he was going to train his dog to sit and fetch and serve him crumpets in bed, and they would go to the park together. And now what? You couldn't do those things with a rabbit, could you?

At first, he tried to resist the fact that the rabbit was very cute because he was hoping, if he looked sad, that Dad might take the rabbit back and get a dog instead. But then he started to feel bad that he wasn't showing the little animal any love. His dad had given the rabbit a name because James wasn't interested, and now the poor thing was stuck with Graham forever! James decided it wasn't Graham's fault he was a rabbit. And he was so tiny, and pretty adorable.

Graham started off tiny anyway, so tiny that he got lost all the time. James and his parents would constantly be looking under the sofa for him.

'You wouldn't have this problem with a dog!' James's mum said – she was a bit disappointed too, although she tried to hide it.

Then Graham started to grow. At first, the Pereras thought nothing of it. But, very quickly, Graham grew to the size of an average adult rabbit. And that was only the beginning. Graham carried on

growing,

and growing,

and growing,

until James found himself googling whether monster rabbits were a real thing.

'I've spoken to the bloke I bought him from,' James's dad said when Graham had reached the size of a Labrador puppy, 'and he says he's a Giant Angora Rabbit. He also says there's no refunds.'

James's dad knew a lot of 'blokes'. He was what adults call 'a bit of a wheeler-dealer', which means constantly looking for new ways to make money. 'Jobs are for suckers,' he used to say, before heading off with a van full of screwdrivers and spanners to sell outside IKEA.

By the time Graham was fully grown, he was far bigger than the dog James had wanted to get. He was still adorable – just massive, as if he was much closer to you than he actually was. Which is why James's legs went numb every night, because that's where Graham liked to sleep.

But this morning James didn't have time to think about his temporary loss of feeling. It was a big day. Uniform on, he shook his legs one more time to get rid of the last of the pins and needles he always got after Graham had been sitting on him, and walked into the kitchen.

On every worktop and surface was a tray of different cakes and pastries – overflowing custard tarts, vanilla slices with cream oozing from their sides, cherry Bakewells with two cherries instead of one, and a large tray full of rhubarb-and-custard doughnuts. James had spent all weekend making them.

Last month, James had got into trouble at school for shoving Darren Brewer, a kid in his class. Darren had been making fun of James because his dad had left, and James lost his temper. He was sent to Mrs Grant, his English teacher, who sometimes stepped in for the school counsellor when he was away.

'This isn't like you, James,' she'd said. 'I know it's been really tough since your dad left. I wonder if it would be good to have something else to focus on for a while?'

'Like what?' James asked.

'Well, what are you interested in? Any hobbies you enjoy doing?'

Feeling a bit embarrassed, James mumbled a response.

'Sorry, James, I didn't quite catch that. You'll have to speak up.'

'BAKING! I LOVE MAKING CAKES, OK?'

Mrs Grant smiled at him. 'Well, that's perfect. Why don't you organize a bake sale for one breaktime next month? I can speak to the school canteen about lending you a table.'

James spent the next few weeks perfecting his recipes, using ingredients his mum had got cheap from the supermarket where she worked. The most difficult thing, he had found, was getting the right amount of rhubarb-and-custard filling into the doughnuts. He had invented this recipe himself, so it took a lot of experimenting.

Last weekend, he thought he'd figured out an

excellent way of putting the rhubarb and custard
in quickly – by using a bicycle pump attached to
an icing bag. It was genius! With just half a pump,
each doughnut was perfectly filled. This worked
so brilliantly that James began to rush. With all the
time he'd saved, maybe he'd also be able to create
another type of filling! Unfortunately, he pumped
too hard on one doughnut, and it flew off the end of
the nozzle and smashed Graham in the face.
Graham was unhurt, but covered in rhubarb and
custard, and he definitely did not like being washed.
That was a tough evening.

After that, James went back to filling the doughnuts by hand.

Today was the day of the bake sale, and James couldn't wait to show the rest of the school his baking skill. He'd started baking cakes as a way of distracting himself and making his mum smile after his dad left, but then he'd really fallen in love with it. He knew he'd never be considered cool, like Alfie Adams or Darren Brewer, but this was his opportunity to make a name for himself at school. To be known for something other than the kid whose dad left. This was *his* moment.

James carried the boxes of cakes carefully out of the kitchen and down the stairs from their third-floor flat, and loaded up his mum's car. He stacked them in neat piles, belting them in place like passengers. There. Now he just had to get them to school.

Unfortunately, his mum wasn't quite as precious about his bakes as James, and as they drove to school (with BoomBox's greatest hits album blasting out of the stereo) James winced every time they hit a bump.

'Mum, can you go a bit slower, please?'

'James, we're actually pretty close to driving at walking speed as it is!' his mum replied.

James groaned. If they did have an accident on the way to school, at least it would be absolutely delicious.

Breaktime came round after what felt like an eternity. James had spent the whole of maths thinking about the best way to display his pastries outside the canteen. The cherry Bakewells on the back left, vanilla slices beside them, yum yums in the next row. The rhubarb-and-custard doughnuts were the star of the show, so they were going right at the front.

As soon as the bell went, James sprinted to the dining hall to set up his stall.

It took him and Sara five minutes or so to prepare, which, James worried, was way too long in a twenty-minute breaktime. As they'd been setting up, they'd missed most of the first burst of kids rushing to the canteen to buy snacks. He couldn't mess up this opportunity. His hand shook a little as he added a final doughnut to the tower at the front of the table.

'The canteen cakes are rubbish!' Sara shouted to people as they passed.

'I don't think we're allowed to say that, Sara,' James said.

'It's marketing, J. They'll understand.'

James took a deep breath. They were ready.

Sara was a whizz at drawing and had made a colourful sign, which read:

And soon people started to come over and take a look. James had chopped up some cakes and put them on a plate for people to try. A Year Ten boy James and Sara didn't know wandered over. He had dark brown hair and thick-rimmed glasses. James held his breath.

'Let's see how bad this is,' he said with a smirk. He grabbed a chunk of vanilla slice from the taster plate and threw it into his mouth. He began to chew really noisily, like he was expecting to spit it right back out again. But he didn't. And he didn't close his mouth, but he did shut his eyes.

James glanced across at Sara who was looking at the boy's open mouth filled with chewed-up pastry in absolute disgust.

'Oh wow,' the boy said finally, after what felt like three solid minutes of chewing. '**THIS IS AMAZING!** Let me get one of each!'

Thick Rims, as James thought of him, seemed to send out a signal to the rest of the kids – they all suddenly started coming over to see what the fuss was about.

'Wow!' said Lucy Clark, a girl from James's history class.

'These are delicious,' said a Year Eight boy with curly brown hair.

'I'll take five of the doughnuts!' said a voice from the back of the crowd.

James and Sara were delighted, and struggled to serve people quickly enough.

As they were hurriedly packing orders, James saw Sara's expression change. She was looking across the playground. Then she said to James the words that would fill him with fear and dread (and a bit more fear):

'OH NO, IT'S ALFIE ADAMS.'

Alfie was the most popular kid in their year. Anything Alfie did, the rest of Year Seven soon copied. He had a shock of blonde hair that grew down over his forehead, which meant he flicked his head a lot to get his fringe out of his eyes. After he'd been doing that for about a week, you would have thought that head-flicking was contagious. Everyone was doing it! Even if they didn't have hair long enough to get in their eyes, people flicked their heads as if they did.

Alfie represented, quite literally, make or break for James's cake stall. If Alfie walked up and bought something, the whole year group, and even some people from other years, would think it was amazing, and James would sell out instantly. If Alfie decided he didn't like the stall, James might as well smash it to pieces and say goodbye to ever being cool or popular for the rest of his school career. Unfortunately, Alfie was also a total bully and liked nothing more than to pick on people just for the sake of it.

Alfie noticed the stall, and immediately walked over, a small group of followers trailing behind him, including Darren Brewer.

'What's all this about, Jason?' asked Alfie.

'Er, it's James. I'm selling cakes and stuff.'

'Why?' Alfie barked.

'Because . . . I, er, like . . . baking?'

James's face suddenly felt extremely hot. He was blushing like he'd never blushed before, and this was only made worse by Alfie and his gang sniggering.

'How can I tell if I want to buy something if I don't know what it tastes like?' Alfie asked, flicking his hair out of his eyes.

His tone made James nervous. *What was he playing at?* Couldn't he see the large plate labelled FREE SAMPLES?

'Well, we, er, have a sample plate,' said James.

Alfie moved over to it. He poked a couple of bits of cake, and James made a mental note to throw those away when Alfie had moved on. Alfie grabbed a piece of yum yum, eyeing it suspiciously.

'This actually looks really good,' he said, and for a moment James was filled with hope. Maybe this was going to be OK after all.

'Thanks, Alfie, I –'

'But I'm not going to eat anything that you and your mum made in your scabby flat.' With that, Alfie flicked the yum yum into James's face. It bounced off his nose and landed back on the plate with all the other samples.

There was a pause. Alfie looked at James, as if

daring him to say something. James stared back, not knowing how to react. What should he say? He really wanted to move that contaminated piece of yum yum away from the rest of the cakes.

Then came the first chuckle from Alfie's gang of suck-ups, followed by a ripple of laughter that moved through the whole queue. And then everyone was cracking up. James looked around wildly. He couldn't see anyone who *wasn't* laughing. Even people who had bought stuff from the stall were pretending it was disgusting and throwing it on the floor.

That was when James knew it was over. Alfie had cursed the stall, and nobody would come near it now. Even the older years, who weren't aware of Alfie Adams's existence, wouldn't risk approaching such an obvious social outcast as Alfie had just marked James out to be – not even for the most delicious cake they'd ever tasted.

'You're such an idiot, Alfie!' The words were out before James even knew what was going on. He couldn't believe he'd said them.

But of course he hadn't.

Sara, hands on her hips, was glaring at Alfie.

'What did you say?' Alfie asked incredulously.

'I said you're an idiot,' Sarah repeated. 'Calling James's flat scabby – you have no idea what you're talking about! And why would you? James would never be friends with someone like you. You don't deserve to touch the plate these cakes are on. Plus, your greasy hair looks like it hasn't been washed in months. *You're* the scabby one.'

You could feel the shock in the air – everyone in the crowd was looking wide-eyed and open-mouthed to see how Alfie would react to this tiny force of nature with pigtails and a furious look on her face. James groaned inwardly. He appreciated Sara defending him, but it wasn't hugely helpful, to be honest. The way Sara had done it felt a bit like your mum sticking up for you.

But amazingly Sara's outburst seemed to work.

'I washed my hair this morning actually, so that shows how much you know,' Alfie said. It was a pretty tame response, and James suspected that was because Alfie was so surprised that Sara had stood up to him. 'Come on,' Alfie said to his mates, and they turned and walked away.

James breathed a sigh of relief. Maybe things weren't so bad. Maybe Sara had saved him. They could sell the rest of the cakes, and his plan would still be on track.

Unfortunately, it looked like Alfie had taken with him any other kids showing an interest in buying anything. James and Sara spent the last five minutes of break with no customers at all, and, as James packed away the last of the rhubarb-and-custard doughnuts, he figured he could say goodbye to his dreams of popularity by cake.

Brukka was sitting in a meeting room at his record label. Across from him were two record-label executives wearing weird outfits. DP was next to Brukka, decked out in his trademark bad suit and trainers. He had his hands clasped in front of him, and he was nodding his head seriously. This meeting was for the record label to approve Brukka's new album, and DP was very nervous about it. Brukka could tell because DP kept slapping his thigh to the music and nodding his head in a really embarrassing dad way.

Just that morning, DP had turned up at Brukka's door in full Lycra, clutching two different energy drinks. He always did things like that when he was anxious.

'What are you doing here?' Brukka asked, eyes blurry with sleep. It was only 6 a.m.

'It's a big day – we need to get energized. Let's go out and get the blood pumping.' DP took a giant swig from one of the cans.

'DP, the meeting isn't for four hours. You've woken me up to stand at my door in the most revealing outfit I've ever seen. I actually think I'd prefer to see you naked. Please go.'

'Your loss, mate. Give me a ping if you want to join me.'

'What's a ping?'

'You know, a ping! A text, a WhatsApp or whatever.'

'DP, can you please stop looking up slang on the internet? You sound insane, bro.'

'OK, playa!' And with that DP speedwalked away.

Now, in the meeting, Brukka looked away from DP, and his eyes fell on the two record execs, who were displaying even less rhythm than DP, shrugging their shoulders and occasionally raising the roof with their arms. The whole room was filled with cringe, and Brukka had no idea how to escape. He was going to suffocate in cringe. A detective would arrive at the crime scene and examine Brukka's body. She would get out her notebook, gather the forensic team around her and say, 'I'm not a hundred per cent sure, but I have a strong feeling this man was killed by an unbearable amount of cringe.'

Brukka's Cringe Crime Daydream was interrupted by the music coming to an end. The record execs stopped moving, but DP carried on clicking his fingers and tapping his feet in an agitated manner, as if listening to some music that none of the others could hear. Brukka did his best to ignore him as he awaited the verdict from the two company people who knew nothing about rap music.

'So, Brukks, I absolutely love this new stuff. It *bangs*!' shouted the exec with hair.

The bald one joined in. 'I think it's really bangy too. Some of the bangiest stuff I've heard in a long time.'

Brukka cringed a bit more. The bald one was just remixing what the hairy one had said.

The hairy one spoke again. 'The only issue is – and listen, I'm just *reporting* this – I played it to my kids. They're twelve and fifteen, so exactly the type of people we should be targeting.'

'Those are the targets. Properly targeted them – **BULLSEYE!**' added the bald one.

Brukka, DP and the hairy one all looked at him – he wasn't even making sense now.

'And what did your kids say?' asked Brukka, knowing that this wasn't good news.

'They said that you sound as if your heart's not in it. It's like you're somebody pretending to be Brukka.'

Brukka thought about defending himself, but the truth was they were right. His heart wasn't in it. He was doing an impression of himself in the hope that he could get away with it. He was almost glad someone had pointed it out to him.

'So I guess the question is,' continued the exec with hair, 'what do we have to do to get your spark back?'

Brukka glanced at the row of screens. He saw all these artists doing their best to look as cool and edgy as they possibly could, but Brukka could see right through them. It was fake. If you wanted to appeal to young people, you needed to talk to young people, work with them. That's what he'd done in the beginning. He'd made music for fun with his friends at school and in the park. They'd helped him come up with ideas and told him if a song was working or not. It had been a collaboration. Maybe that's what he needed to do again. Brukka started to feel excited for the first time in ages.

'You know what?' he said. 'I think I've just had an idea.'

He was remembering a week or so previously. Brukka had been walking through a park because he'd wanted to get some fresh air. He'd been trying to write a new song, but it was completely rubbish. Who wanted to listen to a rap about tea bags? But since he also didn't want to get recognized, he'd decided to wear a Pikachu mask. He was six feet tall, so he did actually get some weird looks from people wondering why a grown man was wearing a Pokémon mask, but he figured it was a lot better than them actually seeing Brukka.

If that happened, he would be swamped with requests for selfies, and people would then ask for funny videos, and Brukka would get annoyed and speed away, and everyone would start running after him, and the next thing you knew a relaxing walk in the park would become a stressful chase through the park. No thanks.

On his walk, Brukka passed a group of kids. They were standing in a circle, rapping at each other about school, about what they were wearing and general affectionate banter. They were surrounded by their friends who were laughing along.

Brukka stopped and watched them for a bit, until the kids noticed the weird man in the mask, and he thought he'd better move on.

As he walked away, he realized that's what he wanted his music to be – free, exciting and not affected by what anybody thought of it.

It was time to mix things up.

At school, the students were constantly being told to 'look for the positives'. And so James was trying very hard to figure out what the positives might be from his breaktime debacle with Alfie.

On the downside, Alfie had laughed at his cakes, and James had wasted an entire weekend baking a load of them.

On the plus side, before Alfie showed up, some people *did* like his bakes, and he also had a lot of cakes and pastries left. Although, now he thought of it, there was no way he was going to be able to eat all of them. Graham probably could, but then he'd end up the same size as their flat.

At lunchtime, James was about to tip all the

stuff into the bin when Mrs Grant saw him.

'What are you doing, James?'

'Oh, I'm just throwing out the cakes we didn't sell.'

Mrs Grant looked confused. 'A sixth-former in my last lesson said your cakes were delicious. How come you have any left?'

'Not sure,' James muttered. 'I just think a couple of the kids didn't like them, and they spread the word and –'

'Oh, James, I'm sorry. Maybe you could make cakes for the staff instead?'

'No offence, miss, but if I start baking cakes for the teachers I might have to wear a disguise.'

'Fair enough,' Mrs Grant said. 'At least give me those ones – the staff will love them, and they shouldn't go to waste.'

'OK. Can we do it secretly, though?'

Mrs Grant nodded and gave him a wink. 'James Perera!' she shouted, drawing the attention of some kids walking past. 'How dare you speak to me like that? The very cheek! I am confiscating these cakes!'

Mrs Grant grabbed them from a smiling James and walked off to the staffroom. At least that would do something to restore James's credibility.

On the way home, James was trying to figure out how to recover from this latest social and professional setback. He was walking through the park where the muffin-man dream was set when his phone buzzed. It was a text from Sara.

Don't worry about today. The cakes were brilliant. You should bake something else straight away to cheer yourself up.
S x

James thought that was a great idea. Baking always relaxed him. He liked the process: the careful measuring, the mixing, the precision timing. But after the day he'd had, it couldn't just be any bake. No. A day like today called for something special. He decided to tackle one of the most fiendishly difficult desserts ever created – the **bread pudding soufflé**.

The bread pudding soufflé was an incredible-tasting dessert that James had once eaten on holiday with his parents. The memory of it made him both happy and sad. The dessert had been absolutely amazing, which made him happy, but it was one of the last memories he had of being with both his parents.

They had been at a posh restaurant in Tenerife. His parents had seemed like they were having the best time ever on that holiday. Every time James looked at them, they were laughing. On the last night there, James's dad said he wanted to take them to a restaurant that had the best desserts, as a special treat. All the food that night had been brilliant, but

James had been focused on getting through dinner so that he could try one of the puddings. At the end of the meal, a waiter wearing an overpowering amount of aftershave came to take their dessert orders.

'My son wants the very best thing you have,' James's dad said.

The waiter smiled. 'That would have to be the ... bread pudding soufflé,' he whispered. 'There is only one serving left.'

'How come that's the best one?' asked James.

'Because bread pudding and soufflé are at opposite ends of the spectrum of baking density!' bellowed the waiter, drawing the attention of the tables around them. 'There is absolutely no way they should be in the same dish, but our chefs have managed to cast a magic spell that makes them work together like poetry. You will eat this pudding and you will cry.'

'I'll have that!' exclaimed James.

The bread pudding soufflé arrived, and it was just as good as the waiter had promised – fluffy and light and creamy. All the ingredients worked together perfectly to create an unbelievable dessert. It didn't quite make James want to cry, but he pretended he was wiping away a tear when the waiter came over to collect his plate.

'I told you!' shouted the waiter as he cleared up. **'Poetry!!!'**

Since then, James had tried to recreate the bread pudding soufflé several times and failed miserably. He had started to call it 'the **DOOM DESSERT**', because every time he made it he would get stressed at how difficult it was and end up with something that tasted awful and looked worse. But that meant this was exactly the sort of thing he should do to try to take his mind off things, as even coming close to getting this dessert right would require every molecule of his concentration. It wouldn't be possible to think about the smug expression on Alfie Adams's face and everybody laughing while he was weighing ingredients and triple-checking the oven timings. And if he finally managed to recreate it, well, maybe today wouldn't end up being such a disaster after all.

Soufflé was a difficult dish anyway, but the bread pudding element made this dessert a similar difficulty level as trying to do a jigsaw puzzle while wearing a blindfold and oven gloves, as someone screams 'Don't do the puzzle!' over and over in your ear.

James tried to recreate it several times that evening. The first one sank, the next was burnt, one was raw and the last one looked amazing but tasted like sugar-coated feet. Each attempt made James more and more angry, but, rather than do something else, each time he just gathered up more ingredients and gave it another go. His mum hated food waste, but luckily they had plenty of the basic ingredients he needed thanks to her supermarket staff discount, and she always brought home nearly expired stuff that the supermarket was just going to chuck out.

On the last attempt, the soufflé actually exploded in the oven, spraying batter all over the inside of the door. When James opened the oven to survey the damage, the smell was so awful that he fell over backwards, recoiling. As he fell, the spatula in his hand knocked the bag of flour off the worktop and on to his face.

'**AAAARRGHHHH!**' he screamed, feeling like he was drowning in flour. He spat a huge cloud of it into the air. Graham watched in silence.

It was then that Mum came through the door. She surveyed the kitchen, looked at her son lying on the floor covered in so much flour you'd think he was ready for the oven himself.

'Oh no, James,' she said, shaking her head.

'What?' spluttered James, sending another flour cloud into the air.

'I know what this is. You didn't have a good day, and now you're making the Scary Dessert.'

'It's called the **DOOM DESSERT**, Mum,' James said glumly. He let out a huge sigh as he got to his feet. 'Honestly, it went so badly. Alfie Adams basically turned everyone against us.'

'How did he do that?' James's mum asked.

James looked at her. He couldn't tell her what Alfie had said – she would be heartbroken. She

worked so hard, and it wasn't her fault that the kids made fun of James for having old trainers, and clothes that other kids' parents had gifted them.

'He told everyone that my cakes taste rubbish.'

James's mum was angry. 'They absolutely do not. Shall I have a word with the head?'

James rolled his eyes. 'Yeah, that would be great, Mum. Then the whole school will know that my mum came in to complain because I didn't sell all my cakes.'

'I see your point. I'm sorry, son. Are you going to give it another go?'

'I don't know. I don't think so.' James hung his head. 'Here, I'll clear this up.'

'No – why don't you go and have a rest? I can take care of this,' his mum replied.

James turned and walked towards his bedroom, with Graham stomping along behind. His mum watched him leave, partly feeling sad for him, and partly feeling sorry for herself as she was going to have to spend the evening clearing up soufflé remains.

James lay in bed, feeling defeated. Ugh, why did Alfie have to come along? It had been going so well! And why did Sara have to make it worse? She shouldn't have said anything. James wished he'd been able to speak up for himself. Maybe he'd have said something clever that would have made everyone laugh and think he was super cool and buy even more cakes. Life at school was going to be a nightmare now. Something told James that Alfie wouldn't let him forget what had happened.

Brukka had been sitting in his car for the past half an hour while the record execs spoke to DP.

'It's an interesting idea,' the hairy one had said. (He wasn't actually that hairy, but Brukka now thought of him like that because he did at least have some.)

'The idea holds much interest to us,' the bald one had said.

'Would you mind stepping outside while we crystallize the idea with DP?' said Hairy.

'Is this because you don't like the idea, and you're going to tell him to talk me out of it?' asked Brukka.

'Of course not! We just want to discuss it,' said Hairy.

'IT'S IDEATION TIME!' said Baldy.

Brukka knew once they started talking about crystallizing and ideation that it was time for him to leave the building.

Brukka looked at his watch. He had been waiting in the car for what seemed like ages when there was a knock on the window. It was DP, waving at him and still wearing his bright yellow sunglasses, even though the day was grey and cloudy. Brukka rolled down the window.

'What's the deal, DP?' Brukka asked.

DP looked flustered. 'OK, so a bit of a weird one,' he began. 'I need you to go in there and tell them you were joking about that idea.'

'Why?'

'Because they really hate it, and I told them I thought you were joking.'

'Why did they say it was interesting then?' Brukka asked, genuinely annoyed.

'Because they're scared of upsetting you. I don't know why you didn't come on that power walk with me! Then this never would have happened!'

'If I'd come on the power walk, I'd have said the same thing in the meeting, but I would also have been dealing with the trauma of being seen out with you in a Lycra onesie.'

Brukka was starting to find this quite funny. DP was not.

'Just get in there and tell them you're joking!' DP shouted. He was breathing heavily. He pulled a protein bar from his pocket and started **CHEWING ANGRILY**.

Brukka hadn't seen DP this worked up in a long time. In fact, the last time DP had been this flustered was when Brukka had turned up late to *The Graham Norton Show*. Brukka hated chat shows – he never knew what to say – but DP told him they were essential.

That day, Brukka had decided to have a little nap before his car came to take him to the studio. Unfortunately, he didn't set an alarm and ended up napping for almost two hours. He woke up to the sound of the driver knocking on his door. He looked at his phone and saw he had 175 missed calls from DP!

He jumped in the car, and they sped to the studio. Brukka didn't call DP because he didn't see the point. He was on his way now, and all DP was going to do was shout at him. When he arrived, DP was waiting at the entrance, looking like he was either going to explode with rage or hug him.

'What the fried chicken, Brukka?!' he screamed.

'I'm sorry, DP – I overslept, man.'

'How can you oversleep for an evening TV show?!'

Luckily, because Brukka was the biggest name on the show, they had waited for him. The other stars – Jamie Oliver, Ant and Dec, and Dame Judi Dench – did the celeb thing of pretending they were fine with Brukka arriving late, but he could tell they were really annoyed.

The show went well, as far as Brukka could tell. Graham Norton made frequent jokes about Brukka being late, and all the others joined in, and Brukka laughed along. When the show finished, Brukka headed to his dressing room, feeling pretty good about things. That was until DP came in.

'What on earth was that?' he shouted, loudly enough for Brukka to become worried that the other guests might hear.

'I thought it went well, man. We made a joke of it,' said Brukka.

'Yeah, well, that's not what they told me. They've said they can't book you again because you're unreliable. Graham Norton was furious.' DP was running out of breath from being so angry.

'He didn't seem furious,' Brukka replied.

'That's what people in entertainment do, Brukka! They pretend to be cool when they're really not.'

This was part of what Brukka hated about the industry. When he'd started, it was just about him making the kind of music he wanted to, and being delighted when people liked it. Now he had to please everyone, and it was impossible to know if that was working because people would pretend to be pleased even when they were angry. Brukka thought it was crazy. And now, with Hairy and Baldy, Brukka was in the same situation again.

'DP, it wasn't a joke, man. And you know I can't go and lie to them. I'm serious – this is what I want to do. And, to be honest, if they're nervous about it, I think that's a good thing – it means I'm trying something different.' Brukka was convinced.

'Brukka, they're saying if you want to go down this road, they might think about dropping you from the label.'

Brukka couldn't believe it. He didn't want to get dropped, but he knew he couldn't go on as he had been – he couldn't create music like this.

'Well, I guess we're dropped then,' he said.

DP took another flustered bite of his protein bar.

'Fine. I just hope you know what you're doing.'

Brukka wasn't sure he did.

James woke up feeling pretty good. Apart from the usual numb legs from Graham sleeping on them all night - obviously. Yes, the bake sale hadn't gone to plan, but he'd read a recipe book late into the night, and he thought he might have stumbled on the way to make bread pudding soufflé properly. The whole bake-sale thing had been quite stressful anyway, and baking was supposed to be fun! He decided he was going to forget all about it, and just bake for himself, his mum and Sara. And if any of it went wrong, Graham could have it. That rabbit would eat **anything**.

On the way through the school gates, he saw Sara talking to Lucy Clark. He wandered over and waited for them to finish their conversation. Every now and again, Sara would glance over and smile at him sympathetically, the way you might look at a dog that had hurt itself.

As soon as Sara finished talking to Lucy, she rushed over to James, her pigtails b^{o}u$_n$c^{i}ng round her head.

'James, we have a new problem. Lucy says that you have a nickname now.'

A nickname. James felt dread pooling in his stomach. He wanted to know what the nickname was, but he also really didn't want to know.

'What is it?' he asked nervously.

'Erm . . . it's Scabby Bake,' she replied.

'Scabby Bake?!

Scabby . . . Bake?

That doesn't even make sense. What does it even mean?' cried James. 'I can just about take people calling me or my flat scabby, but those pastries and cakes were first class!' He couldn't believe it.

'James, I totally agree with you, but I don't think you telling people your baking is "first class" is going to stop the nickname.'

'What do I do then?' James asked.

Sara gave him that concerned look again. 'I think you might have to just . . . live with it until they get bored,' she said.

'How long will that take?!'

This was worse than James had thought. He'd been expecting laughter, jeers, especially from Alfie Adams and his cronies, but to have people saying he was rubbish at the thing he loved doing most in the world was awful. He'd never be able to bake again without thinking about it.

'Well, they've stopped calling Dan Simmonds Wee Pants.'

'He peed in the swimming pool four years ago!!! You mean to tell me that I have to be called Scabby Bake for the next four years?!' James didn't know if he could face this.

'Er, it was five years actually.'

'Oh my God!' cried James. 'Well, that's it. I'm going to have to go and pee in the swimming pool because I actually think I'd rather be called Wee Pants the Second!'

Sara was right. That whole morning at school, James was like the most popular boy in the world. Except instead of everyone cheering and congratulating him and asking him to do more baking, they were all calling him Scabby Bake.

'Hey, Scabby Bake,' or, 'What's going on, Scabby Bake?' and 'Hope you're good, Scabby Bake,' was what James heard all morning. Even one of the teachers, Mr Wilson, greeted him with 'Hello, Sc- James.' *Unbelievable.* The only person who hadn't called him that, and this was only because he hadn't seen him, was the likely inventor of the nickname: **ALFIE ADAMS**.

It was breaktime before James did see him. Everyone was out in the playground. As he was walking around, eating one of the less disastrous soufflés from the night before as his breaktime snack, he spotted Alfie surrounded by a group of kids. There was nothing unusual in that, except for the fact that the kids were gathered like they were watching a performance. Alfie was in the middle of the group, in front of another boy. And it looked like he was shouting at him. But the kid seemed to be enjoying it. And so did everyone else.

James was desperate for a closer look, but he absolutely did not want to get spotted. He'd already had enough *Hello, Scabby Bake*s to last a lifetime.

He pulled up his hood, wondering if he looked a bit like a Jedi, and walked over to the group. Once he reached the crowd, he couldn't believe what he was seeing: Alfie was rapping. And not only that – he was rapping about the kid in front of him:

'Alex, you think you're great,
   coolest kid in the school,
But little did you know we all
   think you're a fool,
Thinking you've got friends and
   your personality rocks,
But people pretend to like you so
   they can play on your new Xbox.
Your hair is a joke, you look like a
   poodle,
And you got little skinny legs
   like noodles.'

Every single time Alfie made a joke about Alex, the group of kids round them would shout and cheer. The atmosphere was **ELECTRIC**.

It was funny and quick, and, as much as James hated to admit it, Alfie was *really* good. James nodded his head, and every time there was a great joke everyone would pump their fists in the air. When Alfie finished, the noise from the crowd was deafening. It was incredible. It was so loud that James thought the teachers were bound to come out and investigate.

As James looked round at the crowd, he thought he saw Alfie make eye contact with him, but he looked away so quickly he was fairly sure Alfie hadn't recognized him. *Phew*. After what seemed like half an hour of the noise, Alex raised his hand and everyone fell silent. It looked like it was his turn! James couldn't believe it. Was Alex about to insult Alfie? This was incredible!

> 'Alfie, the guy who
>   everybody rates,
> But the other day coming into
>   school you was late.
> Mrs Jenkins said, "Alfie, you're
>   late by ten,"
> And Alfie said, "I'm so sorry,
>   I won't do it again."'

The crowd were a lot quieter for Alex. And James wasn't surprised. What was this? Alex was making such soft insults to Alfie! No one was brave enough to properly stand up to him. If James had been up against Alfie, he wouldn't have been so nice. He would have a right go at him. He would talk about his hair, the stupid deep voice he put on, the way he walked like he was always in a music video. James was thinking of all the ways he could insult Alfie and was really enjoying it.

James pulled his hood further down over his face and left. He walked with a little spring in his step. He reached into his pocket and pulled out his phone. He sent Sara a text.

I'm not bothered about the Scabby Bake thing any more – I've discovered rapping

Moments later, Sara sent back the confused face emoji. James smiled and put his phone back in his pocket. It wasn't confusing to him. This was his chance to speak up and be heard finally! To be one of the cool kids, to stop people like Alfie from picking on him. He was going to become a rapper.

At home that evening, two things occurred to James about what had happened that day. Firstly, the bake-stall humiliation wasn't going away any time soon, and, secondly, he was pretty sure he loved rap or grime or hip hop, or whatever it was. He had heard it before, of course, but had never paid close attention. Now he thought this might be something he could become really good at.

He jumped on to the family laptop and started listening to as much grime and rap as he could find. He discovered loads of artists that he immediately loved – Dave, Stormzy, Little Simz. The artist he liked the most, though, was a rapper called Brukka. Brukka's music had taken the world by storm. James had heard some kids at school talking about him, but he hadn't listened to any of his music before.

James put his headphones on and listened to Brukka talk about feeling out of place at school, about his dad leaving his mum and how that made him feel. It was like Brukka was talking directly to James. James half expected a song about how difficult it was to make the **DOOM DESSERT!** His music was clever, funny and full of energy. This was just the kind of rapper James wanted to be.

When James's mum came home, he rushed to the door at the sound of it opening. Mum walked in, dropping her bags like she had been carrying them for months.

'James, I've got you a load of cut-price lemons. I thought you could make some sort of curd –'

'Mum, have you heard of rap music and grime?' he asked excitedly.

'Sorry, James, are you under the impression that I'm ninety-five years old? Of course I've heard of it. I actually used to listen to a lot of it. De La Soul,

A Tribe Called Quest – I went to see a gig of theirs with your . . .' She trailed off.

'With Dad. It's fine, Mum, you can say it,' said James. 'Anyway, I think I really like rap music now!'

His mum smiled. 'How about you play me some of the stuff that you've found, and I'll play you some of the things that I used to listen to?'

And that's exactly what they did. They spent the evening taking turns to play music to each other. James actually liked a lot of what his mum played him, although some of it was a bit boring. James's mum said she liked some of what he played her, but that she couldn't really understand anything they were saying.

'Ooh, I like this one,' she said as they both jumped up and down on the couch, the music blaring out of James's phone.

Just then, there was a knock at the door – a loud knock that didn't seem friendly. It even shocked Graham into running under the table, and he only really moved once an hour.

James's mum answered it. It was Mr Drummond

from the flat below.
He was so pink in the
face he looked like a
giant beetroot, which
started James thinking
about making beetroot
brownies as a treat that
weekend.

'Oh, hello, Ray,'
James's mum said.
'How can I help you?'

'I'm just
wondering how
long you're going to
be playing this awful
music for?' Mr Drummond snarled.

'Oh, I'm sorry – is it disturbing you?'

'It's not disturbing me – it's ruining my evening.
You lot up here are so noisy. If it isn't that monster
rabbit plodding about, it's you playing some awful
racket. I should complain to the council!' He was
spitting a little bit now.

'There's no need for that. We'll turn the music off.'

'If I hear it again, it's the council that will be dealing with it!' Mr Drummond shouted.

James's mum shut the door and laughed a little as she turned towards James. 'Did you see how pink his face was? Come on, let's get ready for bed. I was getting a headache anyway.'

Lying in bed, an idea started to form in James's mind. The rap battle had been an opportunity for Alex to take Alfie down a peg or two, but instead he went so easy on him! If James had had the chance, he'd have gone at Alfie full throttle – rapping about his hair, how he thought he was better than everyone, how he was nowhere near as funny as he seemed to think he was, and also how James had once had a PE lesson with Alfie and when he got changed his feet had really stunk.

James wouldn't normally mention somebody's feet smelling, but in Alfie's case he'd make an exception. James thought he could go on for hours. He could just picture everyone now – cheering him on and punching their fists in the air as he rapped at Alfie.

He grabbed a notebook and started writing it all down. He began slowly with a couple of lines, and then it came pouring out of him. He thought he might end up with an Alfie album. After he'd written all the lyrics he could think of about Alfie, he finished up by writing a song about Mr Drummond looking like a giant beetroot.

The silence in the studio was solid. Brukka and DP had been sitting there, not speaking, for several minutes now. They'd just had an argument. A big one. An argument so massive that Tim the technician had run from the room, shouting 'Save yourself!' at anyone going towards the studio.

'So explain this to me, DP – why are we still on the record label?' Brukka asked.

'Don't you want to be on the record label or something?' an infuriated DP replied.

'That's not the point – you told me that if we went ahead with my idea we'd get dropped. And now we're doing my idea, but we're not dropped. So someone's lying.'

'OK, fine. I lied, yeah?' DP almost sounded scared to admit it. 'I wanted you to abandon the idea and see sense, so I lied to try to help you along the way! But let me tell you this: if this doesn't go to plan – I mean, if the plan doesn't work – we will be dropped!'

'Yeah, well, I don't know whether I believe you any more, DP.'

Brukka didn't understand what the big deal was. His idea was simple – audition young people and kids from around the country to help come up with ideas for new songs and collaborate on his next album. It would mean a lot of work, but, as far as Brukka saw it, many minds were better than one, or two if you included DP, but DP didn't really count because he always said that Brukka's music was great.

The record label and DP thought that it would make Brukka look very uncool, asking kids for ideas on his music.

'Are you a grime artist or a CBeebies presenter?' DP had asked.

They were also concerned about what the press would think. They thought it would seem as if Brukka had run out of ideas and was exploiting children to make money for him. Brukka saw it as getting young people involved, and maybe even finding a young star of the future who he could help take the next steps to stardom.

He'd always trusted DP, who had been with him from the very beginning, but how could he after this? Brukka decided to give DP a test. He was going to deliver the worst rap he had ever done to see if DP would actually be honest with him.

'OK, man,' he said, 'I've actually thought of some fire for the mic, so let me get into the booth and drop this.'

DP lit up immediately. 'That's my guy!' he shouted. 'Let's hear the magic, and I know you'll forget all about this, mate.'

Brukka nodded and made his way into the vocal booth and put the headphones on. If DP was honest with him, he knew he could trust his opinion. If not, Brukka was just going to rely on his own instincts.

Brukka signalled to the engineer to start the music. He nodded to the beat for a little bit, trying to keep the smile off his face, and then started rapping.

'The name's Brukka, and trust me
    I'm no dumb-dumb.
Get off the toilet and then I wipe
    my bum-bum.
Some people have thick hair and
    some hair is wispy,
Some like Coco Pops, and some
    like Rice Krispies.
I like Shreddies, I have them
    before beddy,
And then I lie down and I cuddle
    all my teddies,
Teddy, teddy, teddy, teddy,
    shreddie, teddy, shreddie, dumb-
    dumb,
Krispie-krispie bum-bum.'

He put his headphones down, trying not to

laugh, and made his way out to the seating area where DP was. Tim the technician had just come back into the studio, looking nervous. They were silent as Brukka sat down in front of them. He turned to DP, waiting for his verdict. DP stared at him, as if not knowing what to say. Brukka felt sure he would ask him what on earth that was.

'You know what?' DP said, after what felt like an awkwardly long time. 'That was different, very different, but I think it really works! It's nothing like anything anyone else is doing, and I really think it could push you on to the next level. I think you should call it "Teddy Teddy"! You could actually maybe even bring out an actual teddy or something that people could buy. Don't you think so, Tim?'

Tim the technician nodded half-heartedly. 'Er, yeah, man, really . . . different,' he said.

Brukka looked at the technician, who was just following DP's lead, and then at DP. He loved DP. DP had believed in him when absolutely nobody else did. But, as of this moment, Brukka knew he couldn't trust him.

James readied himself to heave his legs out from under Graham, only to discover that Graham had decided to sleep on the floor. It felt a bit strange to have full use of his legs as soon as he got out of bed. (Though he thought he might actually prefer Graham crushing his knees – it was comforting somehow – but he wasn't going to tell Graham that.) James wandered to the bathroom and was especially pleased to find that he had remembered to charge his electric toothbrush, so his teeth were now feeling absolutely brand new.

None of these things were the reason that James was in such a great mood, though. He felt really good because he kept thinking about all the raps he had written last night. It made him feel amazing, powerful, funny, clever. In fact, he was starting to wonder if this might replace baking as his favourite hobby! It certainly involved less clearing up.

James walked to school with Sara, and even she commented that he seemed particularly happy.

'You OK this morning, James?' she asked.

'Yeah, I'm great. We should probably hurry, though. I think we might be late,' he said, pleased with his rhyme.

This was so easy! Today was going to be amazing. He could just imagine the look on Alfie's face –

'Since when do you care whether we're late?' Sara asked, baffled.

'It's always better to be on time. Your day's

sweet like cake and not sour like lime,' James replied. Sara looked annoyed.

'Why do you keep rapping when you talk? It really makes me regret joining you for this walk.'

They looked at each other for a moment, then burst out laughing.

James was feeling so cheerful today that he didn't even mind the shouts of 'Scabby Bake' that followed him to class. Today was the day he was going to take Alfie down. He even enjoyed maths. He and Sarah had noticed that their maths teacher, Mr Thompson, kept saying 'right' when he spoke.

'So today, right, we're looking at fractions, right? Does anyone know what the bottom number, this number here, right, does anyone know what that number is called? . . . You are right.'

Now that they'd spotted it, James found it impossible not to notice it every time Mr Thompson spoke. Sara's watch had a counter on it, and so they started guessing how many times Mr Thompson would say 'right' in the next minute, and keeping score of who won. It actually made maths much more interesting, and they were counting, so that was maths, wasn't it?

'What on earth is so funny, James?' said Mr Thompson when James had laughed at him using two 'right's in a row.

'Oh, erm, we just thought the subject was funny,' replied James.

'Adding fractions with different denominators?' Mr Thompson asked. 'You think that's funny?'

James lied. 'Er . . . yes?' From the corner of his eye, he could see that Sara was having to look at the floor to avoid bursting into fits of giggles.

'How about we just get on with this, James, and focus on getting these questions right, right?'

At that, James thought his head was going to explode. He was putting so much effort into stopping the laughter coming out of his mouth that he thought it might burst out of his bottom. Next to him, Sara silently shook with laughter.

When breaktime rolled round, he was excited to get outside and see whether another rap battle was taking place. Sara wasn't so sure that this was sensible.

'I think maybe you should wait until the whole Scabby Bake thing dies down. What if Alfie spots you?'

'Exactly! This is the moment to change how everyone sees me.'

'James, I'm not being funny, but no matter how good your raps are you cannot beat Alfie.'

'Well, we'll see about that, won't we?' He did feel nervous, and obviously he hadn't practised as much as Alfie, but this was no time to doubt himself – this was his moment to shine.

James wandered as sneakily as he could to where Alfie was sitting with his disciples. He pulled the hood of his jacket up over his head. There was no rap battle today, though. It was just Alfie talking, and people laughing at what he was saying. James watched for a little bit. He felt pretty good about the raps he'd come up with. He briefly considered walking up and challenging Alfie to a rap battle then and there. But then he thought better of it. Much better to take Alfie by surprise and respond when he was already mid-flow. Then James would have the upper hand. He turned round to go and find Sara.

'Scabby Bake! What are you doing over here?'

James winced. The nickname sounded a lot worse coming out of Alfie's mouth.

'Are you looking for something in particular, Scabby Bake? Maybe your only mate Sara?' Alfie laughed. His pathetic friends laughed along with him. James felt a little whirlwind of anger building inside him. And then, before he even knew what was happening, his mouth started speaking words.

'Actually, Alfie, I came here to ask if you wanted a rap battle.' James couldn't believe he'd said it. He immediately regretted it.

'You're joking, aren't you?!' Alfie laughed. 'You can't rap.'

'I can ... actually,' said James, wishing he'd thought of a better comeback. **'YOU'RE GOING DOWN, ALFIE.'**

There was a stunned silence from Alfie and his crew. James was also quite stunned, despite being the one who was completely responsible for what was happening. After what felt like about six years, Alex stood up, cupped his hands to his mouth and shouted:

'RAP BAAAAAAT-TTTTTTTLL-LLEEEE!'

James looked round to see loads of other kids come rushing over. It felt like there were a lot more than yesterday. His heart started to pound so loudly he thought that other people might be able to hear it. It was one thing coming up with lines in his room, but another entirely to perform them in front of the whole playground. What was he *thinking*? Kids were shoving into him to get close, and he could hear people asking excited questions about who was going to be doing the battling. He felt a hand on his back, and he turned round to see Sara.

'Please tell me that you didn't challenge Alfie Adams to a rap battle?' she asked.

'Er, yes, I think I did.'

Now she looked as nervous as he felt, but then she nodded. 'Right, James. You've got this – and just remember: none of it really matters.' She sounded like she was trying to convince herself.

As the kids formed a circle, Alfie stepped into the centre space. 'I have been challenged to a rap battle by Scabby Bake!' he shouted. This was immediately followed by gasps and chatter from the crowd. 'It will be a very simple one round each,' Alfie continued. 'Crowd noise determines the winner.'

James joined Alfie inside the circle, feeling like he was going into the lion's den. James knew that crowd noise was never going to go in his favour over the most popular boy in the year, but he thought that if he got some good shots in he could at least earn some respect. That was, of course, if he could stop himself trembling and remember what he'd planned to say. It had all sounded so great in his head last night.

'Who wants to go first?' asked Alfie.

'All yours,' said James, thinking that he would

get the advantage of hearing what Alfie had to say before responding.

'OK, Scabby Bake, whatever you say, as long as you think you'll be OK rapping while you're crying.'

James tried to smile to show he was unbothered by Alfie's trash talk, but what actually happened was his lips just wobbled a bit through nerves. It didn't matter. He had come up with enough raps about Alfie that he was sure he could go on for a very long time. Breaktime would end, and James would still be going. They'd have to do a second instalment at lunchtime where Alfie would have to come back and listen to all the other rhymes James had written about him. The rest of the school would cheer James on. He'd be able to restart his bakery stall. He'd be the rapping baker. Everyone in school would know who he was. Everyone in the town. He remembered the dream he'd had the morning of the bake sale. He could be Lil' Muffin!

James's daydream was interrupted by Alfie raising his arm, bringing what felt like the whole school to silence.

Alfie began.

'Can you believe what's
  happening today?
Scabby Bake has got something
  to say.
How does this guy even think he
  can rhyme?
Well, I'm here to show him that
  it's Alfie time.
First of all, what kind of kid at
  our age bakes?
Did anyone here try any of his
  smelly cakes?
Him and his mum spent the
  whole day cooking.
They should have spent their
  time working on how he's
  looking.
Look at his bag, it's older than
  the school,
And his blazer's second-hand.

scabby Bake looks like a fool.
Have a look at his trainers,
   those shoes are pretty rare,
But only because they're the
   ones his dad used to wear.
Speaking of dads, scabby Bake,
   do you know where yours lives?
I heard he ran away cos you and
   your mum are stigs.
Living in your flat that none of
   us have seen,
If you eat anything there, you
   have to get your tongue cleaned.
If this was *Monsters, Inc.*, there
   wouldn't be a scarer
Willing to risk their life to visit
   the Pereras.
Coming here to battle, scabby
   Bake, you must be dumb.
How does it feel to know your
   only friends are Sara and your
   mum?'

At that last line, the crowd went absolutely nuts. There was screaming. People were throwing crisps in the air like confetti. Kids were dancing, even though there was no music. It was a much bigger response than the rap battle had got the day before.

James, however, wasn't worried. Alfie's rap had got a huge reaction, but he wasn't saying anything James hadn't heard before, and, even though Sara looked more anxious than he'd ever seen her, James knew that he'd written much better lyrics. These kids were about to get a shock.

James raised his hand to signal he was ready to begin, and the crowd fell silent. That felt incredible! There were a few seconds of silence while James tried to compose himself. The lines he had spent all evening learning felt trickier to remember now, but he began to work out what he was going to say. Then he stopped. He went to speak again. He stopped. He went to speak again. He stopped.

Sara gave him a little nudge. 'Say something!' she whispered.

OK, right. This was it. He could do it. He was good. This was his new career. This was the start of the new James Perera.

'Alfie, your hair is really flicky . . . it looks really bad . . . I don't like it . . .'

What on earth was that?! James realized he was panicking. He'd written so many great lines last night, but now he couldn't remember any of them. He looked round at the expectant faces. He tried again.

'your hair, it looks awful, makes me sicky.'

It was just when he realized that 'sicky' wasn't really a word that he heard the crowd start booing. It started off as one or two, but, as is often the case with boos, everybody started joining in. Before long, it was deafening.

This was a disaster. This was more than a disaster. This was the kind of disaster that other disasters walk up to and say, 'I thought I was a disaster, but then I saw you. Congratulations.'

There was no coming back from this. Even if James was able to deliver some more lines, he wouldn't be heard over the crowd. They were making a noise like something you'd hear in a Roman coliseum. James glanced over at Alfie, who gave him a smug grin.

It was no good. He'd lost. James turned and walked away from the playground, still hearing the boos even as he went inside.

James ran into one of the classrooms and sat at a desk with his head in his hands. He looked up as the door opened, and then Sara sat down next to him.

James placed his forehead back in his hands. 'You can say it. You can say I told you so,' he mumbled.

'I wasn't going to say that,' Sara replied. 'I actually think it was really brave of you to stand up to Alfie. And it's not as bad as you think.'

James did not agree.

'Sara, the other day I failed at running a bake sale that led to everyone I know calling me Scabby Bake. I look back at that as the good old days now! God knows what my new nickname is going to be - it will probably be Scabby forgot his ... rapping ... bake ...

I can't even think of a good nickname!'

'Look,' said Sara, 'you just need to keep your head down for a bit, that's all.'

'Keep my head down? I'm going to have to keep it in a bag so that people don't recognize me! I'm seriously considering asking if they have some sort of witness-protection schemes for schoolkids who embarrass themselves at **RAP BATTLES**.'

When lessons started, James moved to his classroom with his hood pulled so low over his face that it made it difficult for him to see. He bumped into a couple of people as he was walking through the corridors, but he would rather that than get recognized. Of course, this didn't work once he got to his lesson, and everyone was talking about the rap battle.

'*Makes me sicky!* What does that even mean?!'

'Scabby Bake crashed and burned out there.'

James tried to ignore it all and sank down as far as he could into his chair.

At the end of the lesson, he took his time getting his things together. He wanted to hang back until he would almost be late, and then run to Spanish. At school, the most dangerous times were between lessons when you were moving from class to class. There weren't really any teachers about, so it was a little bit like entering a lawless wasteland. James would have to move quickly and through empty spaces if he was to avoid attack, even if that made him late for lessons.

When he was sure he had waited long enough, James went to leave the classroom. As he did so, Mrs Grant stopped him.

'James, is everything OK?'

'Yes, miss, fine, thanks,' James said quickly.

'I'm not sure I believe you,' Mrs Grant said.

'I don't really want to talk about it, miss . . .' said James. But then he found that he did, and it all came out in a rush. 'Except for the fact that everyone's calling me Scabby Bake after the bake sale, and then I saw Alfie doing a rap battle, and so I decided I like rap music, and I went home and listened to lots of rap, and I thought I could write some raps about Alfie so I could battle him, and everyone would think I was cool, and then I tried to battle him, and the words wouldn't come out, and everyone started booing, and now I have to wear my hood up.' James stopped, out of breath.

Mrs Grant looked at him thoughtfully. 'That's a lot of information to take in, James. But I'll tell you what I think, and you can accept it, and hopefully find it helpful, or you can say "Thanks, miss" and then walk off knowing you're never going to take my rubbish advice. Be . . . yourself.'

'That is what I think I'm doing, miss,' James said desperately.

'Yes, I know,' Mrs Grant replied. 'But being yourself, particularly at school, is extremely difficult. And you're facing the absolute worst end of that. But you have a choice. You can either continue to be yourself and be the wonderful person that we all know you are, or you can let this change you – stop being proud of what makes you who you are. And that would be awful.'

James thought Mrs Grant's advice, to be himself when it was being himself that had led him to become the laughing stock of the year in the first place, was a little bit unhelpful, but he said, 'Thanks, miss,' all the same.

He spent the rest of his classes using his hood for protection, and, when the bell went for the end of the day, he got up and ran straight to the school gates, desperate to escape. As he reached the gates, he saw someone trying to wave at him. At first, he assumed it was Sara because she would be the only person who would want to wave at him. But, as he got closer, he saw it was Lucy Clark. Why would she want to talk to him, particularly now? James stopped, slightly worried that she had just waved him over to call him Scabby Bake.

'Hi, James,' she said.

'Hello, Lucy,' he replied, looking around to see if someone was waiting to pounce on him as some sort of prank.

'I tried one of your cakes the other day – it was **AMAZING**,' Lucy said.

'Erm, thanks,' James replied, checking over his shoulder.

'So I'm having a party on Sunday at my house. I was wondering if there was any chance you might make a birthday cake for it? As well as other pastries and cakes like you did for the bake sale? You'd be welcome to stay for the party, of course. And my mum will pay you. She had somebody sorted, but they got in touch yesterday to say their ovens had broken or something.'

James wondered if she was being serious. 'Lucy, if this is some sort of joke, it's really mean.'

'No, I promise! I really loved your cakes.'

James couldn't believe it. This was completely unexpected. Not only was Lucy asking James to come to the party, she wanted him to make a cake!

Why, though? Surely she knew he was the laughing stock of the school? He shook himself. It didn't matter why she was asking. James had to grab this opportunity. If he made a great cake, maybe he could turn things round. If the cake was good enough for Lucy Clark's party, it would be good enough for anyone. Maybe all was not lost. He might not have to change schools! Maybe he'd even get to try the bake sale again. This was exciting.

'How do you feel about choco salted caramel?' he said, grinning.

James's alarm went off at 7 a.m. on Saturday. He sat up and moved Graham. Graham had gone to sleep on the floor again, but James liked having him on his legs so much that he'd plonked him on the bed the night before. James ran into his mum's room and gently nudged her awake. She didn't stir. He nudged her again. She still didn't move.

What was she playing at? They didn't have time to mess around because they needed to crack on with the baking. He shook her shoulders while shouting 'Mum!' so loudly that Graham started hopping. James's mum woke with a start and scrabbled about for her phone.

'James, it's so early,' she said, reading

the time. 'The party's not until tomorrow!'

'I know, Mum, but we have to allow for failed attempts and taste issues. We're actually already ten minutes behind schedule. We need to start now!'

As James said that, there was a knock at the door.

'Who on earth is that at this time?' James's mum asked.

'It's Sara!' shouted James, running to the door and making Graham hop a couple more times.

James opened the door to find Sara just about managing to stay upright under the weight of flour, cocoa, sugar, eggs and butter she was carrying. She was also wearing an apron that said:

THE CHEF
NEEDS A
HUG

Almost without thinking, a rap formed in James's head and was out of his mouth.

'Chef needs a hug,
     but no need to bug.
Day of baking ahead,
     cakes and pastries but no bread.'

Sara managed to cheer from behind the ingredients. 'See? You are a good rapper. But stop now, and let me in – my mum wanted to buy some bits to support your new business,' she said. 'She says you can pay her back when you open your own bakery.'

'That's **AWESOME**. And maybe I can be the first-ever rapping baker! At least only when nobody except you and my mum are around.'

Lucy had asked for a Brukka cake, which to most people would mean a square cake with a picture of Brukka iced on to it. That was probably what Lucy was expecting too. James wanted it to be better than that, though. After much consideration, he had decided to make a Victoria sponge and buttercream cake model of Brukka, mid rap, holding a microphone made of fondant icing. This meant they would have to create a structure of Brukka in wooden sticks to build the cake around, which would take ages, but it would absolutely be worth it.

On top of this, James had decided that Brukka's trainers should be made of chocolate sponge. This essentially added an hour to the job, which both Sara and his mum tried to convince him wasn't necessary, but he was adamant. This was another chance to get things back on track. He wasn't going to waste it.

In addition, James was determined that every single cupcake, doughnut and square be individually iced with the words 'Happy Birthday, Lucy' and that half of them would be blue and half red. Again, Sara and James's mum told him this was completely unnecessary, but James was insistent, perhaps slightly ignoring the fact that he wasn't working with paid staff but people who had volunteered to give up their Saturday to help him.

'Is now a good time to add the icing sugar?' James's mum said at one point, interrupting James's rap about beating sugar and butter. He stopped mid-sentence and stared at her. Did she not know how sweet all the ingredients she'd just combined were? He needed everything to go perfectly, and he was working with people who seemed to have no idea what they were doing.

'Why don't you just . . . melt some butter, Mum?' he said with a sigh, steering her away from the mixing bowl before she ruined it.

Sara wasn't much better.

'What are you doing?' James asked in horror as he saw her piling so much cake batter into the cupcake cases that when they went into the oven they would rise and merge, creating one enormous traybake. **'STOP!!!!'**

'What's the matter?' Sara said with a start.

When he'd explained, Sara told him to chill out and said that personally she thought an enormous cupcake sounded amazing. 'All right, all right,' she said when she saw the expression on James's face.

She quickly started scooping the mixture out of the cases again. He heard her mutter, 'It's just cake.' She was talking under her breath, but James knew she'd meant him to hear.

At that point, James had to leave the kitchen for a bit to calm down.

When he'd taken some very deep breaths, he returned. He had been working on the Brukka cake alone, as after the cupcake and icing sugar debacles he didn't trust the other two. He was just colouring Brukka's jacket with some edible glitter when he shifted the cake round and – in a moment that he was sure would haunt his nightmares – Brukka's head fell off.

'NOOOOO-OOOOO!!!!!'

He could do nothing but watch as the head rolled on to the floor, under a chair, and –

Right into Graham.

Graham turned his head for a second and immediately went back to his nap, as if reproductions of rappers' heads in icing were things that he saw every day.

Time seemed to stand still for a couple of seconds as James stared in horror. Sara and his mum did too. Nobody knew what to say.

This was awful! The head was covered in rabbit hair and floor crumbs. James would have to remake it. Sara and his mum did try to argue that the head wasn't actually edible anyway, as it was made of polystyrene and icing, so he just needed to pick off the Graham hair and it would be fine, but everyone knows you shouldn't serve a cake that once had fur on it, so James remade the head again from scratch.

They had started at 7.30 a.m. and at 8 p.m. they were finally finished. In every sense of the word. All three of them were exhausted. James and Sara had shouted at each other twenty-seven times, James had snapped at his mum thirty-one times, his mum had told him to be more respectful forty-one times, and James had to leave the room seven times. But, at the end of all that, they had some unbelievable-looking bakes – as well as a huge Brukka cake that might not have looked enough like Brukka that you could recognize him straight away, but if somebody told you it was him you wouldn't argue, which as far as James was concerned was about the same standard as most *Bake Off* contestants. Now all he had to worry about was whether Lucy would like it.

James looked at Sara and his mum.

'I can't tell you how much I appreciate you helping me today. I love you both.'

'Not a problem,' said Sara, 'but, just so you know, I am never, ever, ever baking with you again.'

According to Lucy, 'Everyone goes for brunch on Sundays – it's all over Instagram,' so at 10.30 a.m. James, Sara and his mum arrived at Lucy's house to drop off all the baked goods. There was a terrifying moment when James's mum nearly dropped the birthday cake because Brukka's head was massive – James had to breathe into a paper bag for a few minutes after that – but eventually they made it through with all their heads still in place.

Lucy was the first to open the door. 'James, these cakes are amazing,' she said. 'I cannot believe how great they all look.'

Her mum showed them where to put

everything. 'Did you have help with these, James? They're incredible!'

'Not from anybody who knows what they're doing,' James said jokingly.

Sara gave him a bit of stink eye for that one.

As the other kids arrived at the party, all of them commented on how unbelievable the cake looked, and how delicious the other bits were, and whenever they did Sara made a point of telling them that James was responsible. And it worked because, although the first few people looked a bit shocked, a couple of them came up to James and told him how great his baking was. Without Alfie here, it was just like the start of the bake sale all over again, and people were just munching happily, making occasional '*mmmm*' noises.

James was enjoying the positive reactions to his baking so much that he forced Sara to hover with him by the food, so they could hear all the nice things people were saying.

Peter Leach walked up to the table, looking very suspicious. 'Is it true you made all of this, Scabby Bake?' he asked.

'Yep. And the Brukka cake.'

'What's the least likely to give me food poisoning?' Peter asked.

James groaned inwardly. 'Er, well, none of them will give you food poisoning, but the rhubarb-and-custard doughnuts are my favourite.'

Peter picked one up. He gave James a slightly suspicious look and then bit into the doughnut. He chewed for a second.

'I'll give it to you – that tastes pretty magic,' he said through a mouthful of doughnut.

James grinned at the compliment, but also because, when Peter had taken a bite, a massive splodge of rhubarb had splattered on to his white T-shirt.

Alfie turned up very late for the party. So late, in fact, that James and Sara had started to hope beyond hope that he'd somehow forgotten. When he arrived, James was in the middle of telling the story of Brukka's head falling off. Everyone was laughing, and James was just starting to enjoy himself when he could sense a change in the air. James knew that

Alfie must have appeared behind him because he could see everyone's faces go from relaxed and happy to nervous and scared, as if they'd seen **GODZILLA** emerging in the distance.

'I did not expect to see *you* here, Scabby Bake.'

James really didn't want to talk to Alfie, but it would have been weird to just ignore him, so he turned round to see Alfie smiling his big fake smile.

'He made all the cakes and doughnuts. And the birthday cake.'

As always, Sara had appeared out of nowhere like his bodyguard. James made a mental note to bake Sara whatever she wanted next weekend.

'Oh really?' asked Alfie. There was a hard edge to his voice. 'And is everyone enjoying the cakes that Scabby Bake has made?'

Alfie scanned the room. A couple of people had seen Alfie talking to James and immediately discarded whatever they were eating. Others had incredibly full mouths and were chewing furiously. Clearly, they'd shoved the cakes into their mouths when Alfie appeared – worried they might have to put them down.

'That's great. Good for you, Scabby Bake. Of course, you realize I won't be eating any of it,' he continued, raising his voice. 'I understand Scabby's bakes are all the rage, but the truth is I'd rather not get the plague.' At this, a few people started laughing. 'If you all want to eat his baking, I can't control ya, but don't blame me tomorrow when you all have Ebola.'

More people joined in with the laughter, and James was **FURIOUS**. A whole weekend of hard work swept aside by two lines from Alfie! Sara stepped forward.

'Excuse me, Alfie, I –'

But James stopped her. She looked at him, and he nodded to her as if to say *I've got this*, then he cleared his throat.

'Well, I'm sorry, Alfie, if you don't
   like my cakes,
But the truth is I am excellent at
   everything I bake.
I just wanted to make Lucy's

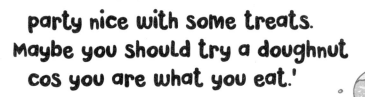

party nice with some treats.
Maybe you should try a doughnut
cos you are what you eat.'

Whoa. Where had that come from? James had no idea, and it was clear by the expressions on their faces that neither did Sara and Alfie. There was a moment of silence before the crowd reacted instinctively.

'*Whooooa*,' said Lucy who'd arrived with more juice just in time to hear James's rap 'burn'. There were murmurs of appreciation all around.

'Incredible line, man.'

'Nice one.'

What would happen next? Had James managed to claw back some self-respect?

Alfie smiled, and seemed to shake his head, and just as James began to smile back, wondering if they might call it quits, Alfie gave him a little push.

It was barely noticeable.

In fact, only Sara and Alfie saw it. But it was enough to send James toppling into the table – more

specifically, the cake table. He fell into it face first, propelling doughnuts, cupcakes and cream slices into the air.

James managed to look up just in time to see Brukka's head rolling towards him.

James and Sara were on a bench at the park near Lucy's house. James's clothes were covered in cream and jam, his face smeared with icing. They sat in silence.

'Well, that was a massive waste of time,' James said eventually.

'You know, apart from the last bit, I thought that actually went really well,' Sara said.

'I don't think anyone's going to remember anything before the last bit!' James said bitterly.

He might as well say goodbye to what remained of his reputation. He was never getting rid of 'Scabby Bake', and now he'd also be known as the kid who fell into the cakes at Lucy Clark's party. Only

Sara would be able to find the silver lining here.

After James had fallen on to the table, he and Sara had decided that it was probably best for them to leave. Lucy had told him not to worry about it, but he couldn't stand around covered in cake, pretending everything was normal – especially with Alfie pointing and laughing at him every thirty seconds. The last thing James saw as he left was Lucy's mum trying to stop their dog from eating Brukka's head.

'I'll admit the cake table crash was not exactly what we were hoping for, but everyone loved the cakes, and people will remember that,' Sara said hopefully. 'You really should stop caring so much about what people think of you. You're great just being yourself – if Alfie and his mates don't get that, it's their problem.'

'Yeah, maybe you're right,' James replied.

Sara stuck her finger into a bit of cake that was glued to James's shoulder and ate it.

'And, on the plus side, you taste delicious!' She laughed.

James smiled. Once again, Sara had made him see the bright side of things.

James walked into his flat to see a horrified look on his mum's face.

'I've only just finished cleaning this place up after all that baking! Er, why are you wearing all your cakes?' she asked.

'We had a bit of a food fight after the party. It was really funny.' James didn't want his mum to worry. He wanted her to think that all their hard work yesterday had been totally worth it.

'Did people like the cakes?' she asked.

'Honestly, they loved them, Mum. Thanks again for all your help.'

James made a seat covering out of baking foil, and he used it to sit in one of the armchairs to tell her all about the party, obviously omitting the bit where he dived into a load of cakes. Then he washed himself off, left his clothes on the floor, despite his mum telling him to put them in the laundry basket, pulled a muscle in his back attempting to give Graham a hug, and tried to take a nap. His mind was whirling, though – Sara was right about him caring too much what other people thought, but he couldn't help it! Maybe he should just go back to hiding away, not drawing attention to himself.

He couldn't stop some new lyrics swirling round his brain too. But when he started to say them out loud, he felt like he couldn't hear properly. He stuck his finger in his ear and wiggled it about, and after a few seconds a small piece of filo pastry fell out.

James was pretty worried about what people would be saying about Lucy's party, despite promising himself last night that he wouldn't care any more. His hood was getting a lot of use. He was walking through the corridor on the way to assembly when a kid he didn't know made a beeline for him.

'I was at Lucy Clark's party yesterday,' the kid said, looking around nervously like he was being watched.

'Oh right,' replied James, glancing around to see what this kid was looking for.

'I just wanted to say, I thought your cakes were so good, and your rap was wicked too. But obviously, you know, don't tell anyone I said that.'

'Er, OK. Thanks.' And with that, the kid ran off.

Great, James thought miserably. He appreciated being told his cakes were good, and it was nice to know that his rapping hadn't been terrible. But what was the point of a few people saying kind things to him in secret if everyone else was going to keep treating him like a loser? *Thanks a lot, Alfie Adams.* For the millionth time since the bake sale, James wished Alfie would suddenly discover he had to move to Australia or suffer a non-fatal injury that would give him a personality transplant.

'Come on,' said Sara, giving James a reassuring nudge as she met him outside the hall. 'Let's go to assembly. That will be a fun distraction.'

Sara was definitely being sarcastic because assembly was possibly the dullest thing you had to sit through at school, far worse than any lessons. The only positive thing about it was that by the time you had sat through the mind- and bum-numbing torture that was a Brazenwell School assembly you were practically ecstatic about heading off to a maths lesson.

This particular assembly had a bit of a twist, however. After Mr Williams had finished showing a photo of himself in swim shorts to make a point about beauty only being skin deep, and Sara had poked James awake three times, the head teacher, Mrs Baldwin, a woman far too nice to be in charge of the school, invited Mrs Grant to the stage to make a very exciting announcement. The school watched the English teacher stand up, ready for her to tell them that the school had new litter pickers or something.

'Some of you may have heard of the grime artist Brukka,' Mrs Grant began, causing the whole hall to start murmuring. 'He's apparently looking for the next generation of rappers, and is holding regional auditions, and Brazenwell is eligible for the South-East heat. It's been all over TikTak the last few days.' At that, all the kids in the assembly hall gave a collective groan.

'His team have given UK schools the opportunity to pick one pupil to represent them in that audition, and the rest of the school is welcome to attend as part of the audience. Anyone wanting to take part in the audition must get a parent's permission and come to see me before the end of school tomorrow. Depending on how many people want to be considered, we will decide how to select our representative. Good luck, all of you, and "respect mine".'

Another collective **GROAN** echoed around the hall as Mrs Grant quoted from a Brukka song. Even James, who liked Mrs Grant a lot, was so cringed out he wasn't sure he'd ever recover.

Mrs Grant, however, wasn't finished.

**'I think you might have it in you
    to show Brukka a thing or two.
I don't want to sound like I am
    a preacher,
but I can rap and I'm a teacher!
Think about it, kids - one of you
    could be a star.
All you have to do is rap a few
    bars.'**

The whole hall was silent, many wincing too hard to even groan. Even the other teachers seemed embarrassed. Mrs Grant cleared her throat, looking a little deflated, and sat down. But once the fog of embarrassment had cleared, the room buzzed with excitement. This was incredible news for two reasons – firstly, Brukka was coming to town, or at least a town nearby, and, secondly, this might be the first time in history that something interesting had been said in assembly.

The obvious question on everyone's mind was: who was going to put themselves forward from Brazenwell? There was Alfie, who on paper was the most likely to end up being the school's entrant, but would anyone else go for it? There was Alex, the kid who had been battling Alfie, as well as a number of others who were known for rapping: Michelle in Year Eleven, a girl who probably knew the most about music as her dad worked in production, and she'd been rapping for ages. Then there was Theo, a quiet kid in Year Ten who had never taken part in any rap battles but who released videos on YouTube of himself rapping in the park. They hadn't had many views, but James had seen them, and Theo definitely had some skills.

Had this happened a week earlier, James would not even have batted an eyelid. But now he felt like he really wanted to give this a go. Sara was always encouraging him not to care what other people thought and just be himself. Maybe this was his chance.

'I know you're going to think I'm nuts,' James said quietly to her as they walked out, 'but I'm thinking of putting my name forward.'

'I actually think it'd be ridiculous for you not to,' Sara replied.

'Really?'

'I think you genuinely could be really good. You'll need to practise loads, but you might be the only person in the world who's good at both baking and rapping!'

'You better not be thinking about putting your name in for this, Scabby Bake.' Alfie had sneaked up behind them.

'Er, well, I, er ... wasn't sure ...' Before James could scrape his sentence together, Alfie stopped and looked him intensely in the eye.

'No, you're sure. You're absolute rubbish, but if the teachers see that you're trying to take part they'll look at it as one of those "helping the little loser kids" projects and put you in ahead of me.'

James thought that Alfie looked unusually angry, and he was feeling very uncomfortable with this whole exchange.

'You don't enter this, and I won't enter when they come round looking for smelly kids who like baking.' Alfie walked away, leaving James feeling miserable.

Of course Alfie wasn't going to just let anyone enter against him. He was the most popular (and, as James was gradually discovering, the most evil) kid in Year Seven.

But a new feeling was taking over James. He was angry. How dare Alfie tell him what to do!

'You're not going to let that little worm stop you from entering the competition, are you?' Sara asked.

'No way,' James replied. 'I'm entering, whatever it takes.'

Brukka looked up at the stage as the next kid walked on. Maybe Philip Nelson would be exactly what he was looking for.

They were hundreds of kids sitting with their parents in the hall. All of them were dressed like rappers. They wore big belts and bright trainers. Some had hats on. Some were wearing T-shirts with their names across the front. Philip was rocking a bright orange tracksuit with matching trainers. He stepped up to the microphone and addressed the crowd.

'HELLO, BIRMINGHAM!'

he said, causing the microphone to hiss with feedback. He took a couple of steps back and continued.

'My name is **SHOCK T**. And this song is called "Rollercoaster" . . .

'Theme park with the fam,
I don't give a damn,
Rollercoaster me and please do it
    quick,
Thrill-seeker gravity, bravest in
    my family.
Let's get ice cream, man, I want
    a lick.'

Brukka sighed heavily. He was starting to think that maybe DP and his record label were right. He was wasting his time. He'd done three heats now, and while some of the kids were very talented, they weren't quite what he was looking for. They all sounded like a rapper that was already out there – each heat would have a Stormzy, a Ghetts, a Dizzee Rascal, a Lady Leshurr and about six Brukkas.

While this was impressive, what he really wanted was to find someone who was doing something original. Someone that made him feel excited about music again.

At the end of the heat, Brukka and DP rushed

to leave before Brukka got mobbed by everyone at the event. They ducked out of the back door of the town hall and headed to Brukka's car, where his driver was waiting with the door open. As he and DP ran towards the vehicle, Brukka saw a kid and his mum standing just a few metres from the car, looking like they wanted to speak to him.

Brukka grabbed DP by the sleeve. 'I think I should talk to them. It'll just take a minute, man.'

DP was reluctant. 'You need to be quick, mate, otherwise we'll be trapped here for hours.' He walked over to the car, already talking loudly on his phone.

Brukka approached the kid and his mum. As he got closer, the boy looked more and more excited.

'It's such an honour to meet you, Brukka – I'm a huge fan,' the boy said.

'Thanks, my brother. How can I help you?'

'Well, it's just that I'm a bit of a rapper, and I want to audition in the South-East heat. I don't know if I'm good enough, but I'd just like to have the chance to show you what I've got.'

'Ah, cool. Well, look forward to seeing you, little man.'

'That's the thing, you see. I want to take part, but there's a kid at my school who kind of thinks he should be the only one to enter, and he made it clear that he didn't want me to audition. But I really want to.'

'Mate, let me tell you something.' Brukka felt for this poor kid. He hadn't had an easy time at school either, and he remembered how much music had helped him escape from it all. 'You need to enter, my man. I'll make sure you have a fair shot. I promise.'

At this, the kid looked like a weight had been lifted off his shoulders.

'Thank you so much, Brukka. This means so much. I didn't know what to do.'

'My man, I look forward to seeing what you've got - what's your name, bro?'

The kid looked up at Brukka, took a breath and flicked the hair from his eyes. 'My name is Alfie Adams.'

James had sprinted all the way home. Their flat was three floors up and James didn't like how the lift smelled, so he had run up the stairs too. When he walked through the front door, he was absolutely exhausted.

'Mum!' he said, panting.

'Yes, James?' his mum called from the living room. She was listening to Magic FM on the radio while furiously cleaning the room. But James couldn't say anything else because he was so out of breath.

'James?' his mum called again. 'Are you OK?'

She walked into the hallway to see him doubled over with exhaustion. Graham was sitting next to him, looking completely unbothered.

James tried to get his story out. 'I . . . want . . . rap . . . but . . . Alfie . . . no . . . want . . .'

He stopped, struggling to catch his breath.

James's mum put her hand on his shoulder. 'Let's get you sitting down and breathing normally, and then you can explain the situation,' she said, concerned.

James went into the kitchen and poured himself a glass of water, taking a minute to get his breath back. He then sat down at the table opposite his mum.

'Tell me everything.'

'OK, you know when I told you that Lucy's party went well? I was lying - what happened was that I'd sort of embarrassed myself in a rap battle with this kid Alfie a couple of days earlier, and I was feeling a bit down about things, and so when Lucy said that she wanted me to bake her birthday cake I got really excited because it meant that I was going to be able to sort of maybe have people like me again -'

His mum interrupted him. 'Sorry, James, did you just say . . . rap battle?'

'Yes, Mum, rap battle, but that's not the point of the story. Alfie turned up at the party and tried to battle me again so I went back at him, and I actually won, like, got a proper reaction, but then Alfie pushed me, and I fell into the cakes, and the Clarks' dog kept trying to eat Brukka's head!' James was out of breath again.

James's mum blinked. 'OK, well, that was a lot to process. Firstly, you shouldn't have lied to me, but I understand why you did. But – why are you telling me about it now?'

James took a deep breath again. 'The real Brukka, not the cake, is running a competition, and he's looking for kids to rap alongside him, and I want to enter, but Alfie told me there's no way I can because I'm not allowed to go up against him.'

He wasn't sure exactly when, but midway through talking about all of this, James detected a change in attitude from his mum. Her face went from concerned to disapproving, and then she looked as though she was almost panicked.

'You shouldn't be wasting your time with all this rap music. It's not good for you.'

James was surprised by her reaction. His mum loved music and had enjoyed the stuff they'd listened to together the other night. Why this change of heart?

'Mum, I really want to do this.'

'I thought you loved baking. And now all of a sudden you're into rapping? I'll always do my best to help you be happy, James, but you've been so distracted lately. I think it's better if you just concentrate on your schoolwork.'

'Please, Mum. I really need your help.'

'I'm sorry, James. I will speak to the school about dealing with this Alfie boy in general, but I'm not letting you enter some silly rap competition.'

'Mum, pl–'

'I said no!' she told him firmly, and James knew that he couldn't push it any further.

'Fine,' he said, and he stormed off into his bedroom with Graham clomping behind.

James stood by the door and waited for Graham to make his way in, which took a long time and sort of ruined his big exit, but he still managed to give the door a good slam.

The next day at school, James had accepted that he wasn't going to be taking part in the rap heats. His mum had been his last hope, and for some reason she'd decided that she was now anti-rap. James was utterly furious that Alfie was going to get his way and probably be the only name submitted to Mrs Grant. He had to do something. If he wasn't able to try to beat Alfie himself, he wanted to make sure that somebody else was going to take him on. Sara was very much against the idea.

'If Alfie finds out you've been encouraging other people to take part, he's not going to be happy.'

'I'm not scared of Alfie,' James said, convincing neither Sara nor himself. 'What do you want me to do? Stand back and just let him get away with it?'

'You're not an Avenger,' Sara said. 'I meant you should enter – not carry out some weird revenge plan!'

But James couldn't enter without his mum's permission. She was bound to find out, and he didn't want to think about how long he'd be grounded for. He was going to have a word with the other potential contenders in the school and make sure they were definitely taking part.

The first person he decided to speak to was Michelle – she was older than him so she wouldn't be bothered by the prospect of upsetting Alfie. The problem was that James didn't know her, and Year Elevens didn't usually enjoy being spoken to by Year Sevens, or, in fact, any other year group, or most people from their own year group. So this was going to be tricky. Also, James didn't really want to let on that he was trying to find a way to take out Alfie in case it got back to him, so he needed to make it seem casual.

He decided that the way to do this would be to

find himself in a lunch queue with Michelle. He had asked Sara to help him with this, but she said she'd rather spend her lunchtime eating crisps and not helping him with what she called 'The dumbest plan you've had since the one where you decided to rap battle Alfie in front of all his friends'.

Getting in the queue behind Michelle involved finding out what lesson she had just before lunch, rushing to get near before she left the classroom, and then following her to the canteen.

At the end of his lesson, James **SPRINTED** straight to the science labs where Michelle would be. He got to the door just as she was coming out, at which point he turned round and tried to act casual, which was difficult because he was totally out of breath from running all the way across school. Fortunately for him, Year Sevens were completely invisible to Year Elevens anyway.

He followed Michelle, making sure he was close enough to be able to jump in the queue straight behind her, but before she got to the door of the canteen she took a left turn and headed away from it. Oh no! Could James have made a huge oversight here? Yes, yes, he had. He watched as Michelle reached into her bag and pulled out a packed lunch. How could James have not prepared for the possibility that she brought her own sandwiches?

There was no way he was going to be able to speak to her now. A Year Seven absolutely could not even sit near a Year Eleven eating a packed lunch, much less have a conversation with one. He watched Michelle sit down with her friends outside and felt a little pang of despair. He couldn't just walk away from this empty-handed. And it was then that James had his rubbish idea. Literally.

He ran to the canteen and paid someone at the front of the queue to buy him a bag of crisps. Then he walked over to where Michelle was sitting, stuffing the crisps into his mouth. As he got close, he finished the crisps, scrunched up the packet and pretended to try to throw the bag into the bin, but aimed straight at Michelle. Unfortunately for James, he wasn't very good at throwing, and

he actually got it straight into the bin. He had
to improvise.

'Oh God, sorry. Did I nearly get you?!' he
blurted out.

'What?' Michelle clearly didn't know what he
was talking about.

'The crisp packet. I just threw it in the bin.'

'Yes?'

'I thought I might have hit you with it.' This wasn't going well.

'Er ... OK.'

'You going to do the rap thing with Brukka?' James asked, trying to sound casual, but failing miserably.

'What's it to you?'

'Oh, just because, er, I heard some people were ... scared to go up against Alfie Adams in Year Seven.'

She stared at him, incredulous. 'I don't get scared, especially not by piddly little Year Sevens. I'm entering.'

'OK, cool. Bye!'

James walked away very quickly, as if to try to escape the awkwardness. He almost bumped into Sara, who had been watching.

'Just wanted to let you know that was *smooooooooth*,' she said, laughing.

As conversations went, it had been truly dreadful. But he'd got what he wanted from it. Michelle was going to enter. James was happy with that. He was so happy, in fact, that he decided not to approach the other kids that might have wanted to be involved. Sara was right – it had been awful with Michelle; he was terrible at this, and he really didn't fancy doing it again, especially as he'd already got a result.

James was feeling pretty pleased with himself for the rest of the day. Or at least until he turned a corner on his way to his last lesson and spotted Mrs Grant standing outside his classroom. It looked very much like she was waiting for him.

Unluckily for James, it turned out that Michelle's younger brother was in Year Seven and one of Alfie's cronies. As soon as James had completed what he thought was a very subtle investigation, she had gone straight to speak to her brother who had gone straight to Alfie and told him everything. Mrs Grant had been standing nearby and overheard the whole conversation.

'James, I think we need to have a chat.'

Mrs Grant motioned for James to follow her into an empty classroom. She gestured for him to sit down, and then took a seat opposite him. She looked slightly saddened.

'James, you need to start telling me what's going

on. Why haven't you put your name forward for this competition?'

James told Mrs Grant about Alfie warning him off entering, and begged her not to say anything. He told her that he'd spoken to his mum, and what she had said, and finally he told her he'd got desperate and tried to make sure that at least somebody else was going up against Alfie.

Mrs Grant looked thoughtful. 'OK, well, this is all quite complicated, but I really think you should just enter if you want to. It seems like you're really passionate about rapping.'

'Alfie wouldn't be happy about that,' he said.

'Don't you worry about Alfie. I've already spoken to the judges, and they're letting us have two entrants from the school for the competition. Michelle isn't actually eligible for the contest because she just turned sixteen, and that's the cut-off point in terms of age. I've explained that to her – she was a little disappointed, of course, but she understands. No one else has put themselves forward so it will just be you and Alfie. If he gives you any trouble about it, you come straight to me. And I'll speak to your mum as well – I might be able to help her see it from your point of view.'

James went home absolutely buzzing.

Weirdly, his crisp-packet plan had actually helped, so maybe he was a genius after all. On the other hand, perhaps he could have achieved the same result if he'd just spoken to Mrs Grant in the first place. Either way, he was thrilled that he was going to get to perform in front of Brukka.

When the kids shuffled into assembly the next morning, James was so excited he could scream. **He was still in with a chance!** He had phoned Sara the night before to tell her the news, and she had to ask him to tell her again because he was talking so quickly she said it sounded like Spanish. He'd been bursting to share the news with his mum, but, after the way she'd reacted when he'd first told her about the competition, he decided to keep quiet and let Mrs Grant handle her. Instead, James whipped up some delicious raspberry chocolate brownies to celebrate. They were the best ones he'd ever made – gooey and still warm from the oven. He'd brought some into school to share with Sara.

James would have skipped into the hall if that wouldn't have meant being absolutely ridiculed by everyone else in the room. Also, he didn't think that Stormzy would accept a BRIT Award by skipping up to the stage. On second thoughts, James decided that walking would be fine. As he went to sit down, he saw Alfie, who gave him the filthiest of filthy looks. It didn't matter, though. Even Alfie Adams couldn't dent James's mood this morning.

Before the announcement, James had to sit through a presentation on a recent school visit to Hastings, in which the history teacher, Mr Powell, used William the Conqueror conquering England as a metaphor for schoolwork and triumphing in exams. James thought this was difficult advice to take because you can't shoot a maths test in the eye with an arrow, although he really wished he could.

Finally, it was time to hear about the Brukka competition.

Mrs Grant stood up to make the announcement. 'You will remember that on Monday I told you about the exciting opportunity for someone to represent this school in a talent search being run by the rapper Brukka. Well, we have news.' James thought he might explode with excitement at this point. 'I am delighted to announce that Alfie Adams will be representing Brazenwell Secondary School in the South-East heat.'

With that, a huge cheer erupted from the hall, and the suck-ups sitting with Alfie patted him on the back and did that '*braap braap*' thing really badly.

James felt blood rush to his face. His head was spinning. What had happened? Was this part of the plan? Was Mrs Grant keeping him a secret so that Alfie couldn't get to him?

He looked at Mrs Grant, hoping for reassurance. But she just gazed back at him with such sadness that James knew immediately he wasn't taking part.

Alfie had won.

Brukka was sitting on a rooftop. Around him were about thirty different types of snacks, biscuits and cakes, and they were all attached to fireworks. *How on earth have I got myself in this situation?* he thought.

DP had insisted that he take part in a series of TikTok videos with the influencer Cheese. Cheese had **four million** followers and had managed to achieve that in only a few weeks. He posted videos where he would review different foods and toys. If they were good, he would nail them to the 'Cheeseboard of Fame'. If they were bad, he would smash them to pieces, or shoot them with something, or blow them up. Cheese had earned his name by eating a Babybel at the beginning of every video. He had posted at least one video every day for a year, which meant he had eaten at least 365 Babybels. Brukka wasn't sure he'd eaten that many in his entire life.

DP had convinced Brukka that doing a video with Cheese would be good publicity. Apparently, Cheese's last video of him smashing a thousand meringues with a baseball bat had been viewed over twenty-three million times. Brukka asked if he should just blow up a trifle in his next music video, and DP told him he was being difficult.

And so here he was – on a rooftop about to launch a jam doughnut into the sky. He normally loved jam doughnuts, but this one was horrible.

'So why are you not feeling the jam doughnut, Brukks?' asked Cheese with a touch too much energy for Brukka's liking.

'There's not enough jam, and the doughnut is stale – both baking crimes.'

'HAHAHAHAHAHAHAHAHAHAHAAH.'

Cheese was laughing way too much at what Brukka

had said. 'You are mad for that one, Brukka. OK, let's light it up. When I say go, you let it go. GO!'

Brukka lit the firework attached to the jam doughnut. Seconds later, the rocket **SHOT** into the sky.

'See you later, doughnut!' shouted Cheese as it flew into the air, leaving a jammy trail behind it.

As they watched it go, they heard a voice from below. It was DP, who was with Hairy and Baldy from the record label. They were very excited about Brukka connecting with the 'TikTok youth'. DP was wiping jam from his suit as he shouted up to Brukka.

'Hey, man, how's the Cheese?' he asked.

'We're about to move on to cheesecake,' Brukka called down.

'Ah, great – we might move a bit further away because we're getting quite a lot of cake debris on us!' said DP.

Brukka sensed he was nervous. 'What's going on, DP?' he asked.

'Just chatting to the guys here, and we were wondering about when you were going to bring the auditions to an end and get back to the album?'

Brukka had expected this, and he didn't blame them. He still hadn't found anyone and was worried he might be wasting time that he could be using to work on new songs.

He sighed. 'OK, let's cancel them, but can I just do one more?'

DP was silent for a few moments as another jam doughnut **WHIZZED** past overhead.

'Brukks, this has to be the last one. We do this and then we go and finish the album, OK?'

'Yeah, man, course.'

He probably wasn't going to find a young person now, and, even if he did, why did he think that was going to make any difference to his music? He had constructed this whole plan on a sort of gut feeling, but now it all felt utterly insane. Maybe his career was over. Despite all this, Brukka knew he had to make sure that final audition went ahead because, even if it all came to nothing, he had made a promise to Alfie Adams.

James ran to Mrs Grant's classroom where students were queuing for the first lesson of the day. He was hoping to get to her before class started, but he was willing to demand the lesson stop so he could speak to her. He wouldn't really, of course – that would be absolutely terrifying – but he was angry enough to pretend that was something he might do.

Mrs Grant saw him approach as she was about to let the students in. He half expected her to avoid him, but she looked at him, resigned, as if she knew what was coming. She sent the class into the room, and James was talking before he got to her.

'What is going on, miss?! You told me not to worry. You betrayed me!' he said.

'Keep your voice down, James, and don't be so dramatic. I did not betray you. It's complicated.' Mrs Grant was annoyingly calm.

'How? You lied to me!' James knew he was being rude, but he didn't care. She *had* betrayed him, regardless of what she said.

'I know, James, but I didn't mean to. Let me explain. Yesterday afternoon, after I spoke to you, I fully intended to enter your name, but I can't go around making plans without keeping your mother in the loop. It wouldn't be allowed. I phoned her to get consent, and she refused. She wouldn't give a reason. I did explain that you really wanted to do it, but she was adamant.'

James couldn't believe what he was hearing.

'She must have given some sort of reason. I know she didn't want me to do it, but I thought if you explained it to her ... Mum's always telling me to do what makes me happy!'

'I'm sorry, James,' Mrs Grant replied.

Suddenly James had to get away. He turned and stormed through the corridor, ignoring Sara, who called after him. He'd never felt so angry in all his life. These were people who said they cared about him. He couldn't really blame Mrs Grant – she was only following the rules after all – but he would never forgive his mum for this.

James wanted his mum to know how angry he was so he was practising different poses for when she came home from work.

At first, he tried standing with his hands on his hips, but when he posed in the mirror he realized it sort of looked like he was about to start a dance routine. Then he decided to sit on the floor and wait, but he got pins and needles in his legs and had to move. When he got up, his left foot was completely dead, and he nearly fell on Graham. Then he wondered about moving a chair from the living room into the hallway to sit on, but decided that was too much effort. In the end, the best option seemed to be to just wait in his room.

He lay on his bed, listening to a Brukka album and reading about the best way to make a light egg custard. When he heard the front door open, he jumped up and sprinted to the door. He didn't see Graham, who was lying across his bedroom doorway.

'WHOOOOOOAAAAAAAA!!!!'

He didn't quite fall over at first, just sort of stumbled, but the momentum meant he kept

running and stumbling and trying not to fall – almost in slow motion – until gravity won, and he fell to the floor in a mess of arms and legs right at his mum's feet.

He looked up at her. 'I'm really angry with you,' he whimpered.

'James, are you OK?' his mum asked, concerned. 'Is this about the rap competition?'

'Why don't you want me to do it?' James said, untangling his legs and getting up.

'It's complicated,' his mum replied. She looked really troubled.

'Mum, I want to do this so much. I love rapping, and I think I might be good at it.'

'I think you could be good at it too, but I just feel that, rather than going off and competing with Alfie Adams, and trying to impress this Brocky person, maybe you should practise and work on your routine at home. I'll give you whatever support you need. You don't have to enter a talent competition.'

'Mum, **this is massive!** Brukka is looking for someone to work with him! I'm never going to get an opportunity like this again, and I probably won't even end up winning, but I just want to have a chance!' James was desperate now. He couldn't understand why his mum was being like this.

'Look, there will be plenty of other opportunities for you. I just don't want you doing this competition, OK? I don't think it's a good idea.'

'But why, Mum?' James wailed.

'Because I'm your mother, and I say it's a bad idea,' she said through gritted teeth.

'But *why*, Mum?'

'Because that's what I think, James.'

'*But why, Mum?*'

'James! Enough!' his mum shouted. James stopped in shock. He had never heard his mum shout before. 'I don't have to explain myself to you! I am your mother, and I've told you that you're not allowed – so just leave it!'

James lost his temper. 'I can't believe you, Mum!' He was shouting too now. 'All I want to do is have a go at something I love, and you're saying I can't – for no reason! Do you know how awful it is to be the laughing stock of my year? People saying my clothes look old; people telling me I'm weird because I bake; people calling me Scabby Bake! It's horrible.'

James could see his mum was getting upset. Her face had turned red, and her eyes looked watery. But he couldn't stop. She'd ruined the biggest opportunity of his life. Before he knew it, he said something really nasty.

'You know what? I bet Dad would have let me! I wish he was here instead of you!'

His mum looked devastated. She turned away, unable to speak.

James paused, knowing he'd gone too far, but he didn't care because he was too angry.

He turned, ran to his room, forgot that Graham was still there and tripped over him again.

Sara was sitting in her bedroom, listening to Brukka. She was trying her best to like it, but she really couldn't. Everyone at school loved this type of music, and if everyone liked it so much there must be something to it. She couldn't find it, though.

She grabbed her phone and stopped the album. She scrolled through Spotify and found something she preferred: Metallica. She clicked on a song and started headbanging to the music. She was headbanging so loudly that it sounded like her head was knocking. Then she realized that someone was knocking at her bedroom door. Her dad shouted through it.

'Sara! You have a visitor! Oh, and great song!' He loved heavy metal.

Sara stopped the music and ran downstairs. Standing in her hallway was James.

'Hi, Sara. I'm really sorry to bother you, but I was wondering if I could stay tonight?'

'Yeah, of course! That'd be great,' Sara replied, though she was slightly distracted by a couple of things. One of them was the fact that James seemed pretty upset. The other was that he was holding the handles of a wheelbarrow. And in that wheelbarrow was Graham.

James had been staying at Sara's house for the last couple of days. His mum knew where he was, and Sara's parents knew that they'd had an argument, and said they were happy to have him. When he wasn't at school, he would wander around their house in Sara's *Frozen* dressing gown, looking sad. Graham was back with James's mum because she'd decided that looking after both James and the planet's largest rabbit was a bit much to ask of Sara's parents, but James hadn't spoken directly to his mum since the argument.

Sara was struggling with two things: getting James to talk very much while in this monumental sulk, and also not laughing at the sight of him mixing ingredients while wearing her dressing gown. She eventually realized that the only way to get James to open up was to do things wrong, and so she started deliberately messing up his recipes and forcing him to help her as a way of distracting him. He did seem marginally happier when telling her that she was going to ruin his cake by adding the flour too quickly.

James and Sara were ready to put what James had called 'Sara's mistake' in the oven when Sara's mum came into the kitchen.

'Mrs Grant is at the door,' she said. 'She wants to talk to you, James.'

James was utterly baffled as to what this might be about. He looked at Sara who just shrugged. He went to the door with zero clue as to what Mrs Grant might want. He was still feeling pretty grumpy with her, even though he knew she was only doing her job.

'Hello, James,' she began. 'Er, I hear you've not been yourself recently.' She looked him up and down, and James remembered that he was still wearing Sara's *Frozen* dressing gown and pink *Encanto* slippers.

'Who told you that?' James asked. He glanced towards the kitchen and saw Sara duck behind the door.

'Ah. Well, yeah, my life is over, miss,' he said.

In years to come,

Alfie Adams would have the number-one-selling album, and in interviews he would talk about that record being inspired by an absolute loser kid from his school who had since been crushed to death by a giant rabbit. James was interrupted in these thoughts by Mrs Grant speaking again.

'Good to see you've got a healthy perspective on the situation, James. I wonder if this might cheer you up. The local primary school are after somebody to teach a group of Year Fives to make flapjacks as part of their weekend baking club, and I put your name forward. I told them about your baking exploits! They're happy to pay you and said they would recommend you to other schools if it goes well. It's happening tomorrow afternoon so, if you'd like to do it, you'll need to start preparing right away. I wanted to tell you the good news in person. The details are here.'

With that, Mrs Grant pushed an envelope into James's hand and said goodbye.

James didn't know how to feel about this. He still loved baking, and he loved telling people what to do. But, all the same, he really wasn't in the mood for teaching some kids how to make flapjacks, not when he knew that just down the road Brukka was probably changing Alfie Adams's life without ever getting to see James rap.

He sighed. Perhaps it was time to accept that nobody would ever know what a good rapper he was. But if he was good at rapping, he was GREAT at baking. And all of a sudden James wanted to make sure he did a really good job.

Sara and James were in her kitchen, practising different types of flapjack. James was explaining the art of flapjacking to Sara.

'Obviously, your basic flapjack is easy. But a strawberry flapjack with yoghurt topping is more difficult because the strawberry changes the consistency of the mix, and so you have to be careful you don't ruin it.'

'James, no offence, but I don't think Year Fives are going to really understand if you explain it like that,' Sara said.

'Oh, I know, which is why I've written a flapjack rap,' James said proudly.

'You're kidding,' Sara replied in disbelief.

James cleared his throat.

'Excuse me for clearing my throat,
But I have to explain that you
  need large oats.
You can use porridge oats if you
  like,
But don't use instant as that won't
  be nice.
How careful should you be?
  Well, I would say very
When you're making flapjacks
  that involve strawberry.
Melt the butter in a pan until it is
  fluid,
And stir it up with a wooden spoon
  as if you were a druid.
Mix the honey and the oats plus
  the sugar golden,
Then tip the strawbs and the
  butter into the bowl that you're
  holdin'.

Use the back of the spoon to
    flatten the mix in a baking tray.
Bake for forty minutes, wash up
    while you're waiting.
Hey, how easy was that?
    I told you it was nothing.
Make sure you let the flapjacks
    cool before you start cutting!'

As James ended the rap, he held his arms up in the air like he'd finished a gig. Sara applauded wildly.

'You know that was actually brilliant?!' she cried.

'It wasn't brilliant, Sara. It was a rap about flapjacks.'

'That's why it was so brilliant!' Sara said excitedly. 'Remember when you were at the party? What made you beat Alfie was that you didn't overthink it. You just rapped about baking, and it worked! That's what you should focus on!'

'Nobody actually wants to hear raps about baking,' said James, looking at Sara as if she'd lost the plot.

'I do! It works because you're rapping about what you're really passionate about,' Sara said. 'Why don't you do one about something else to do with baking? What about that soufflé you can never get right? The **DOOM DESSERT.**'

James was unconvinced, but, after thinking for a minute, he gave it a go.

'Souffle is tricky, but you don't
    know tricky
Till you've tried it with bread
    pudding and made your hands all
    sticky.
I've tried 137 times to make it.
My hand was mixing so hard I
    thought I'd break it.
Of those times, I reckon three
    were edible,
And the rest I'd genuinely rather
    have sat and ate vegetables.'

Sara laughed at the last line, and that made
James laugh too.

'What did I tell you?' she said.

James had actually impressed himself there, but
he still thought that Sara's idea was crazy. Surely
nobody wanted to hear raps about pastry!

Brukka was about to get into a bin. Yep, that's right – **a bin**. Word had got out that he was going to be at the town hall today. There were hundreds of people surrounding the building who had been there from the early hours of the morning. Some of them had even camped overnight. He could see them yawning as they packed up their tents, and one man was shouting to his neighbour **'OI, THAT'S MY POLE!'**

They needed to find a way to get Brukka inside without him being swarmed. After five minutes of quality brainstorming, DP had come up with what was probably the world's worst idea. And that was why Brukka was standing in front of a giant wheelie bin.

'DP, I'm not sure about this, man,' said Brukka doubtfully.

'I wouldn't expect you to be sure about getting into a bin, mate, but we haven't got time to argue!'

They'd stopped Brukka's car about half a mile from the town hall. A huge wheelie bin had been brought over, and now Brukka was about to climb into it, before being wheeled by one of his security staff to the venue.

This was all well and good, but Brukka had a couple of issues. Was this bin going to be clean? He didn't want to trundle half a mile in a smelly bin. And why did it have to be that far away? What happened if someone saw him getting in or out of the bin? There were too many funny headlines that could come out of that:

BRUKKA GETS BINNED.

BRUKKA HAVING A WHEELIE, WHEELIE BAD DAY

Brukka was still asking questions when DP forced his head down and **SHUT** the lid. It was actually quite nice in there – DP had organized a little pillow and some snacks and drinks. Initially, Brukka wasn't sure about having a bin picnic, but then he noticed there were jam doughnuts.

As the bin neared the town hall, Brukka could hear people chatting excitedly. He held his breath in case they might be able to hear him. He really didn't want to get spotted in there. He was sure a photo of him eating a jam doughnut in a wheelie bin would go viral.

There must have been some sort of step into the back of the building because the guy pushing it took five attempts to get Brukka inside. He would get halfway, and then drop back, making a loud bang every time he did so, causing Brukka to yelp. It must have looked funny because Brukka could hear some of the crowd laughing. At one point, the lid popped up and Brukka caught a glimpse of all the people waiting to get in although, thankfully, they didn't spot him. This was mortifying. Eventually, the guy managed to get him over the step, and Brukka was in the building.

He took the box of jam doughnuts with him as he got out of the bin and headed to his judging desk. He wasn't expecting much from today. But he'd promised Alfie Adams he'd be here, and he wasn't going to let him down. He remembered all too well the bullying he'd experienced in school. If he could help a kid like Alfie in any way, he would.

He'd watch these kids, say his thank-yous, and then go and figure out what on earth he was going to do next. He had no idea how he was going to get out of this funk. He felt totally uninspired. He was wondering if he might have to leave his record label, go away for a bit and think about the sort of music he'd really like to make, instead of the music that DP and the label managers wanted him to.

He'd have to have a difficult chat with DP after this event. He wouldn't be happy, but Brukka had to be true to himself. And maybe, just maybe, he might be inspired by one of the rappers today. Maybe Alfie would be the person he was looking for.

James was starting to feel a bit nervous as he went up to the building where Mrs Grant had told him to go for the baking club lesson. He had begun to remember what Year Fives were like and was having visions of getting flapjacks **HURLED** at him by a group of ungrateful kids.

He walked round to the back doors of the town hall as Mrs Grant's letter had told him to. He thought he might be going mad with nerves because, as he made his way up the path, a man walked past him pushing a wheelie bin, and James could swear he heard a voice coming out of it. He was so distracted by this bin voice that he didn't notice the crowds of people queuing to get into the building or the music coming from inside.

He reached the doors and gave them a loud
knock. After a few moments, a huge man opened
them. He was wearing a black suit and had an
earpiece in. James had no idea why flapjacks would
require this level of security.

**'WHAT'S YOUR
NAME, LITTLE
MAN?'** asked the man
in a voice so deep that
James felt it rumble
his chest.

'Erm, James. Perera.
I'm here about the
flapjacks.'

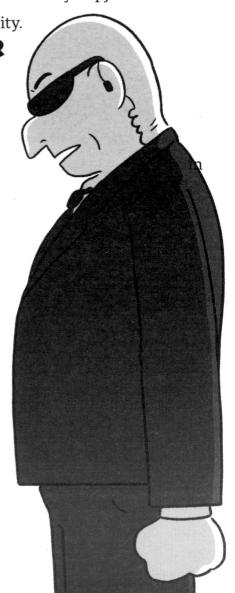

The man gave him a confused look and then checked his tablet.

'Yep – got you. Do you have any guests?' he asked.

'Guests?' James was utterly baffled.

'For the show?'

'The show?' James said, feeling like maybe the wheelie bin had been a sign he was going mad after all.

The huge man was starting to get impatient. 'The audition, show, whatever.'

'Erm, no,' replied James.

'OK, follow the signs to the dressing rooms, and someone will come get you shortly.'

James had absolutely no idea what was going on, but he decided to follow the signs anyway. He walked through a bustling corridor full of security staff and what looked like engineers working on microphones and talking to each other via earpieces. He thought his brain was going to implode, but then he saw a large sign that read:

WELCOME TO THE BRUKKA AUDITIONS! HE CANNOT WAIT TO MEET YOU! GOOD LUCK!

What on earth was going on? James took his phone out of his pocket and called Sara. She answered excitedly.

'It's amazing, isn't it?!!!!' she screamed.

'What's going on?' replied James, putting the phone to his other ear.

'Tell me you've figured it out. Mrs Grant was lying! She entered you for the audition!'

'But what about my mum?' James asked.

'She knows! She's here with me now!'

'Where?' James asked, only just starting to accept what was going on.

'We're waiting to come in. The queue is **MASSIVE!**' Sara shouted, deafening James's other ear. Then James heard a new voice.

'James?' It was his mum.

'Mum! I can't believe this. Why did you change your mind?'

'I realized how important it was to you. I'm sorry that I stood in the way of your dream. We can talk about it more later, but for now go and have fun. And remember, whatever happens today, I love you.'

'Yes, Mum, thank you,' replied James.

'James, go out and absolutely **SMASH IT!**' It was Sara again.

'But, Sara, I haven't had time to prepare!' James said, feeling a weird mix of nerves and excitement flowing through him.

'Look, you perform better when you don't have time to start doubting yourself. Remember Lucy's party? Just believe in yourself, and it'll be brilliant. I know it will.'

James knew she was right. 'Listen, you guys can come backstage if you want – I'm allowed guests!'

'Hold on,' said Sara, and James heard a muffled conversation between her and his mum.

'Your mum says she wants to stay in the crowd and support you from here. But I'll come find you.'

'OK,' said James. 'I'll give them your name.'

James went up to one of the security people and asked her to let Sara in when she turned up backstage. The woman nodded and said something into her wrist.

James tried to calm himself down as he walked to the dressing rooms. As he wandered through the corridors, he could see all sorts of kids dressed like rappers. He looked down at what he was wearing. He had on an old tracksuit and a rucksack containing twenty-seven copies of a strawberry flapjack recipe. He wasn't exactly rap-ready.

He came to a room that was labelled

GREEN ROOM

There was a list of all the rappers underneath: **JIGGA T**, **ZEPHYR**, a double act called **ANT AND WRECK**, **JAMES PERERA** and the one name he really didn't want to see – **ALFIE ADAMS**.

James walked into the green room and sat down. He was worried that he might be a bit underprepared so he stared in the mirror, planning his performance. Just as he entered deep thought, someone came through the door. Expecting Sara, he looked up. But it wasn't Sara. It was Alfie.

He was wearing a green hoodie and matching trainers. He had sunglasses on top of his head, and his hoodie was tucked behind a silver belt buckle. Alfie took a seat opposite James and smiled at him.

'Was there something you wanted, Alfie?' James asked.

'Nice outfit,' said Alfie with a sneer. 'You look like you're headed to the library.'

'You look like a green,' said James, trying to insult him back, but knowing that made absolutely no sense.

'I told you not to enter this thing, Scabby. But I knew you'd try something to mess this up for me. So I had to take measures.'

'What measures?' asked James. What did Alfie mean? That couldn't be good.

Alfie grinned slyly. 'Well, you see, I was talking to Brukka about how much of a bully you are. How you warned me off taking part in this competition. About how you turned everyone at school against me. And he believed every word.'

James opened his mouth in complete disbelief, but nothing came out. There was no way Alfie could have managed this. Had he actually spoken to Brukka? But Alfie looked too pleased with himself for this to be a lie.

'Nobody wants you here, Scabby Bake. You might as well go home.'

The town hall was packed with Brukka fans and supporters of the kids taking part in the audition. DP was pacing up and down at the back of the hall in a bright pink-and-yellow suit, shouting into his phone and waving around a can of Monster energy juice. Brukka sat at his desk, surrounded by security.

The first act up was **JIGGA T**. He was a small boy wearing a tracksuit and gloves. He picked up the mic and began to rap.

'Jigga Jigga T like L, M, N, O, P.
I spit a hot rhyme, then drink a
    cup of tea.

Then I do a wee, wash my hands
carefully,
Then sit down to watch something
on TV.'

Brukka found Jigga T quite funny, but he felt
like all the kids auditioning were just imitating other
rappers. He totally understood why they were doing
that, but he wanted to find someone original that
could spark his love of music again.

Next up was **ZEPHYR**. He was a very tall

child, probably taller than Brukka. He was so tall that for a moment Brukka half wondered if this was a twenty-five-year-old man pretending to be a child. He rapped almost exclusively about how tall he was.

'I'm zephyr, and I'm taller than anyone you know,
your dad, your bro, I'm taller than those,
I'm taller than your teacher, I'm taller than a cook,
I'm taller than a stack of a thousand books.'

After Zephyr was a double act called **ANT AND WRECK**. They were brother and sister and were wearing complementary tracksuits. Ant, the brother, had a white tracksuit top and black bottoms, and Wreck, the sister, had a black tracksuit top and white bottoms. Brukka liked how they looked. Their song was about animals. And they rapped in alternate lines, starting with Ant:

'speed of the puma,
smart like a fox.'

'charge like a rhino
and as strong as an ox.'

'Ant and Wreck, rare
like a platypus.'

'Rhymes that reach
everywhere like an octopus.'

Brukka liked them a lot. And they would definitely do well if they released a single. Brukka could see DP watching them and nodding his head excitedly. They certainly had potential.

The next kid up was **ALFIE ADAMS**. Alfie stepped onstage with the confidence of somebody who was already a rap artist. He could have been filming a video. Brukka was taken by the response from the crowd. You'd have thought this kid was already famous by the way the audience responded to the announcement of his name.

Brukka looked around the room and saw kids wearing T-shirts that said **A DOUBLE**, Alfie's rap name. He couldn't believe it – Alfie already had fans. He certainly didn't seem like the shy boy that Brukka had met before.

Alfie looked to the side of the stage and nodded for them to put on his backing track. There was a click in the speakers, and suddenly Alfie and the beat started in perfect synchronicity.

'A Double, that stands for
    Alfie Adams.
No manners here, forget your sirs
    and madams.
I drop raps like monkeys drop
    bananas.
I could beat everyone here while
    still in my pyjamas.'

The crowd was going wild. This kid had stage
presence, striding up and down the performance
area with the audience hanging off his every word.
He even started signalling for the crowd to jump up
as he spat his rhymes into the mic. He was getting
the kind of response that Brukka would have been
pleased with.

From the side of the stage, James watched Alfie's performance. It looked like a proper gig. Alfie was getting the crowd to throw their hands in the air, and they were doing it! Alfie was strutting up and down the stage like Brukka himself.

Alfie finished his verse at exactly the same time as the beat finished and then dropped the mic. There was a clang and a whistle of feedback as it hit the stage. For a couple of seconds, there was silence. And then there was an **EXPLOSION OF NOISE** as the crowd went wild. Alfie stood with his arms folded, nodding his head. You could see him thinking: *The record deal is in the bag.*

James had a sudden urge to run away. He was up next, and Alfie had given what you could only describe as an unfollowable performance. There was no way James was going to get anything like that kind of response from the crowd.

Sara, standing behind James, read his mind. 'Don't worry, just do your thing – you'll be fantastic,' she told him.

James wasn't so sure. He wished he'd had time to practise. No, now that he was here, he wished he was in that flapjack lesson. What had he been thinking? Of course he couldn't do this. Alfie would win. Alfie always won.

One of the backstage staff tapped James on the shoulder, interrupting his thoughts. James looked round.

'Perera, **YOU'RE UP NEXT**.'

James felt his stomach fill with nerves. His legs were shaking like the jelly in a sherry trifle. Was he about to go onstage and completely freeze? Was he going to cry? Maybe he would spontaneously combust with embarrassment.

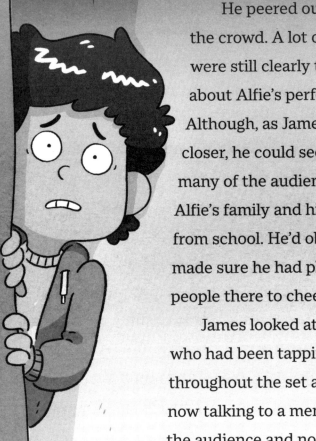

He peered out at the crowd. A lot of them were still clearly talking about Alfie's performance. Although, as James looked closer, he could see that many of the audience were Alfie's family and his friends from school. He'd obviously made sure he had plenty of people there to cheer for him.

James looked at Brukka, who had been tapping his foot throughout the set and was now talking to a member of the audience and nodding in agreement. James imagined the person saying how incredible A Double was. He felt absolutely awful.

Suddenly a voice boomed through the hall tannoy:

'Please make some noise for our next auditionee – **JAMES PERERA!**'

James didn't move. He couldn't. There was no way he could go onstage now. He felt Sara's hand on his shoulder.

'Go on, James. You've got this,' she whispered.

'I really don't,' James replied.

'I disagree,' said Sara, and gave him a shove.

James stumbled out onstage in front of the crowd. They responded with applause. Not the rapturous applause that had greeted Alfie as he stepped out. It was more like the sort of applause that you might hear when someone plays a good shot in a cricket match. *Not really the sort of thing you'd want to hear at a rap concert*, James thought glumly. He looked out at Brukka, who was staring back at him keenly.

This was it. He was no longer thinking about this as an opportunity now, but more as an experience where he had to try to avoid humiliation. He gave a nod to the sound tech at the side of the stage to start the track; there was a click and the beat started.

For about ten seconds, James froze. He opened his mouth, but **NO SOUND** came out. He had forgotten everything. The beat sounded like it was being played through porridge, and his legs were shaking with nerves. Oh God, was this going to be his performance? Was this what he'd begged his mum so desperately for? He might just have to signal for them to stop, and then walk offstage, head straight to an airport and spend the rest of his life in Zimbabwe.

As he wondered about how he'd get on in Zimbabwe, he gazed into the crowd and saw his mum staring back at him. She looked a bit worried, but she was also smiling and mouthed the words **'YOU CAN DO IT!'** James couldn't let his mum or Sara or Mrs Grant down. He'd put them all through hell, and they'd never stopped supporting him. Even if there was no chance he'd get to perform with Brukka, he was going to give it his very best shot.

'Hello, everyone! My name . . .' James paused.

What name should he give? All the rappers had really cool names; James Perera was a bit boring, but his only nickname was Scabby Bake, and he definitely didn't want everyone calling him that forever.

James couldn't believe he'd decided to try to come up with a new name right now, but all of a sudden it came to him. He remembered what Sara had said to him, that his best raps were about baking because it was his favourite thing in the whole world. He didn't have to listen to Alfie call him Scabby Bake any more – he could be whoever he wanted to be. He thought back to the day of the bake sale, the day he'd discovered rapping and had his very first run-in with Alfie Adams. The day that had started with a dream about . . .

He could hear Sara clearing her throat at the side of the stage and realized that the audience was still waiting for him to finish his sentence.

'Hi, everyone. My name is Lil' Muffin!'

He heard a couple of boos from some of Alfie's friends. His knees really went then, and once more he considered running offstage, but then he looked out into the crowd and saw his mum again. Mrs Grant had joined her now.

James steadied himself.

He raised the mic to his mouth and started to rap:

'I bake cakes that make Greggs
   quake.
There is no limit. I have no
   brakes.
Muffins and doughnuts and
   gateaux with no nuts,
I rap about baking while you all
   shake your butts.
I have no interest in what most
   kids do,
In fact, most kids say to me
   "I don't like you."
The only pleasure I get comes
   from baking surprises.
Some people like Xbox, I enjoy
   vanilla slices.

some people know things like
    how to make friends,
Whereas I know how to stop jam
    coming out a doughnut's back
    end.
you'll hear most people rapping
    about being a hard nutter,
But I rap about how to blend
    flour with butter.
A lot of rappers talk tough, but
    they're fakers,
Whereas I know how to be the
    world's best baker!'

He looked across at Sara again, and she nodded
to him to encourage him to carry on.

'When I say "vanilla", you say
    "sponge"!
vanilla -'

About five people responded with 'SPONGE!'
It was hardly a deafening cry. But, in that moment,

James could have gone up to each and every one of them and given them a hug. It also gave him enough courage to try another one.

'When I say "Lemon", you say "meringue"! Lemon!'

This time, most of the audience shouted, **'MERINGUE!'** – even some people wearing A Double T-shirts.

James finished the chanting, held his hands in the air and then dropped the mic to signal the rap was over. The applause was much louder than he'd been expecting. Maybe it wasn't quite as loud as for Alfie's set, but people had still enjoyed Lil' Muffin's raps, and James hadn't let himself be intimidated by Alfie. That was all he wanted.

James looked at Brukka, who was smiling at him. Had he liked it or was he just being kind? James glanced across at Sara, who was beaming and gave him a double thumbs-up. At the side of the stage,

James could see Alfie laughing his head off. James knew Alfie would sneer at him for rapping about baking, but who cared what Alfie thought? James had wanted to rap in front of Brukka, and he'd done it – he'd really done it! And people had liked it. Whatever happened now, he was glad he'd come.

Brukka was absolutely buzzing. He had spent countless hours waiting to find some sort of inspiration. He had defied his record label and his manager, DP, and he had seen hundreds of acts. And then – all of a sudden – he had found exactly what he was looking for. Somebody amazing. Somebody who could make a difference in music. Somebody who Brukka was going to record a single with and help with their music career. He needed to speak to this boy immediately.

He grabbed his notebook from the table and ran through the hall, dodging people clamouring for photos. He made his way to the backstage area. He was genuinely excited. He ran down the corridor and knocked on the green-room door. The door opened, and the kids who had auditioned were sitting around the room. In his excitement, Brukka had forgotten he would have to see all of them.

'Er, hello, everyone,' he began. 'This audition has been mad good – easily the best one we've had so far. Each and every one of you is an amazing talent, and you should all carry on doing this. On your way out, my manager, DP, will take your email addresses. We'll be in touch about each of you getting a free day of studio time to make your own single. You all have incredible potential. Could I ask you all to step back out on to the stage with me, please?'

As Brukka walked onstage, the group was hit with a wall of sound from the crowd. The noise was deafening, and Brukka waited a few moments, soaking it all in and looking round at the kids to see their reaction before raising his hand to get the audience to be quiet. He lifted the mic to speak.

'Thanks so much to everyone who came today. **YOU'VE BEEN INCREDIBLE.**'

Every time Brukka ended a sentence, the crowd started screaming again, which meant it was taking him a really long time to get through what he needed to say.

'I started this process a while ago. My record label thought I'd gone mad. And so did I, to be honest with you. But today I found someone who I think has made it all worthwhile. Someone who embodies why I thought this whole search would be a good idea. So I would like for you to show some love ...'

While Brukka was talking, Alfie began to make his way to the front of the group. They all stepped aside for him. James felt a poke in his back as Alfie pushed past him to stand almost next to Brukka in time to be announced as the winner.

'PLEASE GIVE IT UP FOR LIL' MUFFIN!!'

The crowd went **wild**. James applauded for a few seconds before wondering why everyone was looking at him. He saw Brukka beaming at him with his fist outstretched for a bump. James couldn't believe it. Brukka had really said his name! The truth started to sink in, and James returned the bump. The noise from the crowd grew even louder. He could see Mrs Grant and his mum hugging each other and jumping up and down. He felt someone shove past him roughly and turned to see a furious Alfie storm off the stage.

Brukka led James offstage and through a corridor into his private dressing room. The room was filled with the smell of aftershave, and there were about six of every chocolate bar and soft drink you could buy on the table. There was a Bluetooth speaker in the corner playing tunes by Brukka, which meant that he liked to listen to himself. James thought that was a bit strange, but he didn't really have time to process it as he was trying to figure out exactly what was going on. This must be a case of mistaken identity. Surely Alfie had been better? And Alfie had told Brukka that James was a bully – why would he want to work with him?

Brukka sat down opposite James and looked at him thoughtfully.

'You're amazing, man. Amazing.'

James was in shock. Could this be real?!

'Seriously, I have watched so many kids, so many young people, and they've all been excellent, but you, you're something else. You were yourself. I mean, baking! *Baking!* Who on earth would rap about baking? But that's you, and you did it. You were yourself - authentic. But you made it fresh. Mate, it was **SICK**.'

James was astounded. 'But I thought Alfie got a better reaction,' he said croakily.

'Alfie's talented but you're unique. You have something I haven't seen in anyone. Ever. Let me tell you something - you did you. You weren't trying to be something you're not. You're not even dressed like a rapper. You look like you're ready to go to church! Your name is Lil' Muffin! But then you start rapping, and everyone loves it. You remind me of me when I first started making music.'

'Mate, we are going to get into a studio. We're going to make some baking tunes. And then I'm going to make some of my own tunes telling my truth! You've inspired me, man.'

'I thought you might hate me – because of what Alfie told you about me,' James said.

'I'll be honest, little man: I thought you were a bully. And I came to have a word with you about it in the green room – I wanted to make sure you weren't going to give Alfie any hassle. Instead, I heard Alfie telling you what he'd done – how he lied to me. I let him have his moment onstage. He was good, man – proper good – but I can't work with a bully.'

James smiled with relief. What a day! He made a mental note to bake Sara her favourite red-velvet sponge cake to thank her. If it wasn't for her insisting he stay true to himself, he wouldn't be in this room with his hero, and wouldn't have the opportunity to change things for him and his mum. James wanted to scream with excitement, but Brukka might think he was a weirdo.

There was a knock at the door. Brukka got up

excitedly. 'Ah, man, this will be my manager, DP. I can't wait for him to meet you. He wasn't sure this whole thing was worth it, but now he can say hello to the reason it definitely was – you.'

James's head was whirling as Brukka made his way to the door. He could not believe this was real. He was expecting to wake up any second now, but then his thoughts were interrupted as the door opened.

'James, this is my manager, DP.'

James looked over. There, standing by the door, were Brukka and his manager. His manager had a weird expression on his face. For a split second, James couldn't work out why and then all of a sudden it became completely clear. It also became very clear why his mum had not wanted James to take part in this competition.

Brukka's manager, DP – or Dev Perera – was James's dad.

'Hello, James,' said DP.

James didn't say anything. He had pretty much shut down. It was weird enough that Brukka had just told him he was amazing. What that moment absolutely didn't need was to get even crazier. And then he'd discovered that Brukka's manager was his dad. How did this even happen? He hadn't heard from his dad in years, but he still couldn't believe that he didn't know about it.

'Have you two met before?' asked Brukka, immediately sensing the weirdness in the room.

'Yes, Brukks, this is my son, James.'

'What?! You're kidding! This is mad! Nah, this isn't mad, this is destiny!'

'James, I realize this must be a huge surprise . . .'

James did not know what to say. He was in shock. This was too much for one boy to process.

'Look,' his dad continued, 'this is a lot to take in, and I don't think there's any point getting into it all now. I'll be honest – I'm a little bit in shock myself.'

Ever since his dad had walked out, James had practised what he was going to say if he ever saw him again. He was going to tell him how difficult he had made it for his mum. He was going to explain how little money they had. He was going to make him understand the sense of rejection he felt when his father decided he wasn't worth sticking around for.

Unfortunately, in none of the scenarios that he'd practised was his dad the manager of the biggest rapper in the country. And part of him was glad to see his dad again after all this time. It was really very confusing. James tried to say something, but instead of words what came out of his mouth was a very quiet croaking sound, so quiet that James wasn't even sure he was making it.

'Are you OK, little man? You're making a weird noise.' Brukka looked concerned. 'Look, why don't you stay here and relax for a bit – help yourself to chocolates and stuff, and I'll have a chat with DP. You probably want some time with him too, so we'll figure all of this out. OK?'

James nodded.

'OK, great,' Brukka said. 'We'll be back in about ten minutes, James. And seriously, my brother, well done – you're a special talent.'

DP smiled nervously at James, and James smiled nervously back. And then they were gone, and James put his head in his hands and tried to stop his head from spinning off his neck.

James was still sitting with his head in his hands when the dressing-room door opened and Sara flew in. As soon as she saw the table of treats, she raced over and ate three chocolate bars in quick succession.

'What are you doing?' James said.

'Just say you've eaten them. Brukka won't deny his child prodigy some chocolate snacks,' Sara replied.

'Sara, I've had two! When he comes back, I'm going to have to tell him I've gobbled five!'

There was a knock at the door. Brukka and his dad must have finished their chat.

'Come in!' James shouted. James gestured to

Sara to hide, and she dived behind the sofa, grabbing another chocolate bar as she went.

The door opened, and in walked Alfie.

'Oh, I thought this was Brukka's dressing room,' said Alfie sheepishly.

'It is, but he's stepped out to talk with his manager.'

'OK. I'll go find him.'

'OK.' James was puzzled. Why was he trying to speak to Brukka?

Alfie started to walk out of the room and then stopped.

'I just wanted to say, I'm happy that Brukka chose you,' he said.

James was taken aback. 'Really?' he asked, surprised.

'Yeah, because now the whole world is going to see how pathetic you are. You're rubbish, Scabby Bake. I genuinely hope you flop, and that, because Brukka chose you, he flops too, and then I'll see him on the way down when I'm on the way up.'

James sighed. He'd heard it all before from Alfie,

and he was really starting to find it a bit boring.

'Alfie, I couldn't care less what you think. You lost, and you can't hack it. You laugh at me because of my clothes and because I like baking, but you're just a bully, and you must be pretty unhappy to be so horrible to people all the time.'

With that, James picked up a Crunchie, raised it above his head and let it fall to the floor, imitating a mic drop.

For the first time in his life, Alfie was speechless. He opened and closed his mouth a few times, searching for something to say, but, in the end, he just glared at James and then walked out.

Sara gave James a double thumbs-up over the top of the sofa.

There was another knock at the door, and James's dad walked in.

'All right, J!' he said, smiling.

James had forgotten that's what his dad used to call him. A flood of warm, nostalgic memories filled James's head. His dad teaching him how to ride a bike, going to McDonald's for dinner, making his dad a cake on his birthday and his dad saying it was the best thing he'd ever eaten.

'So, listen,' DP continued, 'we love what you did out there, and Brukka thinks you're a star. He would really like to do something with you as soon as possible. We're doing some recording next week. We'd like you to join us, but it would mean missing a bit of school.'

'Right. Well, I'd have to ask Mum.'

At the mention of James's mum, DP's face broke into a bigger smile.

'How is she?' he asked.

'She's good. She's a bit stressy,' James replied, then felt like he shouldn't have said that. DP laughed again.

'Yeah, she is. She's very stressy. I can't imagine she was very happy about you doing this competition, was she?' James hoped his face didn't give away the answer. 'Well, tell her this is more important than school, and we'll meet you at the hotel before we head to the studio. I'll text you all the details.'

James nodded. 'Can I say thank you to Brukka, please?'

'He wanted to come back, but a fan spotted him, and he's been mobbed. But trust me: he's very excited about working with you.'

James practically skipped out of the room and down the corridor. He was nearly at the exit when he remembered that Sara was still hiding behind the sofa.

James headed back to Brukka's dressing room to rescue his best friend. He wasn't sure what he was going to do, but he knew he couldn't just leave her in there. He walked to the door of the dressing room and pulled out his phone to text her.

Is there anyone in the dressing room?

A reply came back almost immediately.

No, I decided I'd live here behind the sofa. Of course there are people in here.

Brukka is talking to some man called DP.

James leaned against the door so he could listen to what was being said.

'Why have you picked him?' DP was almost shouting.

'DP, that's your son you're talking about. For the first time ever, by the way. I didn't even know you had a kid!'

DP sounded embarrassed. 'I haven't mentioned it because things ended pretty badly with his mum. I cannot believe that you've chosen him over that Alfie kid!'

'That's why I'm an artist and you're the manager, DP. Alfie was good, really good, but he's got nothing original about him. I've heard it all so many times before. Have you ever even heard the word "gateaux" in a rap tune before?'

'No, and maybe that's because rapping about baking is ridiculous!'

'If you ask me, you're not seeing things very

clearly right now,' Brukka said, sounding serious.

There was a pause and what sounded like a long sigh from DP.

'So I definitely can't convince you to work with this Alfie kid instead?'

'No, man, I'm telling you - your son is the one!'

'Great - well, this is a big mess, Brukks. Now I've got to explain to him why I left. Thank you!'

James and Sara walked behind James's mum and
Mrs Grant, not saying a lot. James could see that
Sara was having trouble thinking exactly what to
say.

James's mum and Mrs Grant paused further
ahead. As he and Sara approached them, Mrs Grant
said, 'Well done again, James! You should be very
proud.'

'Thanks,' James said, feeling his cheeks warm
a little.

'I'm heading off now – see you both in school!'
Mrs Grant said, beaming.

They waved at her, and James turned to his mum.
'I'm going to walk Sara home, if that's OK,' he said.

'Of course – and thanks for being there today, Sara,' his mum said.

James and Sara walked on in silence. Once they reached her house, they stopped on the doorstep.

'I'm so sorry, James. Those things DP – your dad – said. It wasn't cool. What are you going to do?' Sara said, finally voicing what had been in her mind the whole way back.

'I don't know. The whole reason I did all this was to make something of myself. Now I have the chance, and I have to walk away because my own dad doesn't believe in me?' James could feel tears pricking his eyes, but he didn't want to cry in front of Sara.

'James, you're so special. You're one of the most kind-hearted and honest people I know. You don't need to prove yourself to anyone. If you don't want to do this, then don't.'

'Sara, I haven't ever told you this, but you're the best friend that anyone could ever ask for. Thank you for being amazing.' James went to walk away, but then turned round and gave Sara a long hug.

Whether he took her advice or not, he wanted her to know that he appreciated her.

When James got home, he found his mum waiting anxiously for him.

'James, I'm so sorry – I should have told you that your dad was his manager, but I didn't think you'd actually get anywhere near Brukka. I also want you to know that I'm so proud of you! You were unbelievable up there. I was shouting so loudly!'

SPONGE!

James laughed. 'Thanks, Mum,' he said.

'So what happens now?' his mum asked.

'I don't know. I really don't.'

James told his mum about how Sara had been trapped in the dressing room, how he'd heard his dad telling Brukka he didn't want to work with James. James's mum listened attentively. When he was finished, she told him her story.

'I never said this to you before, but the reason your dad left was because he kept going on about living this exciting life. He said that having a family shouldn't stop you from doing interesting things. He said I'd changed since we'd had you. That's the whole reason he got Graham. He thought that a dog would be a bigger inconvenience than a rabbit. Then Graham got massive. One night he told me that he wanted to get rid of him. But I knew it wasn't about Graham. It was about settling down with a family. He didn't want to be held back by commitment. He asked me why I didn't want my life to be exciting. And I told him that seeing you live your life and become everything you want to be, James, was exciting enough for me. And then he was gone. I never saw him again. Until today in the hall, of course.'

James took this in, feeling a heaviness in his chest for a moment. Then he gave his mum a hug.

'The problem I have, Mum,' he said, 'is that although Dad is clearly an awful human being, Brukka isn't. And he wants to work with me! But I don't want to work with Dad! What do I do?!'

James's mum smiled. 'James, if you want to go and make your rap dream come true with Brukka, then don't let your dad hold you back. You should do what your heart tells you and don't let anyone, including me, stop you. Why don't you sleep on it?'

James kissed his mum and headed off to bed, completely unsure what to do.

The next morning, there was a knock on James's bedroom door.

'Come in!' he shouted. He'd lain awake for ages, wondering what he should do, before falling into a deep sleep. And his mum had been right. He'd made his decision.

James's mum opened the door to find James standing in a full tracksuit and sunglasses, his arms folded rapper style. Graham was by his feet, completely oblivious.

'Ah,' she said. 'I guess you've made your decision. I'll speak to the school to see if you can have a couple of days off.'

Without saying anything, James pressed a

button on his phone, and a beat started. James's mum looked baffled.

'Mum, I'm really sorry that my
   dad was a nightmare,
And that he left us cos he really
   don't care.
I'm also sorry that I have been
   tricky,
Baking every weekend, making
   the kitchen sticky.
Thank you for bringing me up on
   your own,
And thank you for helping me
   bake without a moan,
And thank you for spending your
   days in a job you hate,
Just so you can pay for all the
   food that Graham ate.
There is no way that I would walk
   out on you to go and make music
   with Dad. That's not cool.

I can't really believe he wants
   me to miss school,
Although people call me "scabby
   Bake", so maybe I'm the fool.
So, Mum, let me tell you
   something quite simply,
If I'm exciting enough for you,
   then you're exciting enough for
   me.'

James finished and raised his hands, almost expecting a crowd to go wild, even though he was just in his room with his mum and Graham.

As soon as he finished, his mum burst into tears before running over to him and giving him a huge hug. She squeezed him so hard that he started to struggle to breathe.

He gasped. 'OK, Mum, that's enough, thanks!'

'Well, not that I was expecting you to make that decision, but we do actually have some baking to do,' his mum said. 'A friend of mine has asked for a Pikachu birthday cake, and they're paying decent

money, so we have to make it extra special.'

'Perfect!' said James.

There was a knock at the front door. James ran to open it. It was Sara, carrying a load of baking supplies and yellow fondant icing.

'I don't know why I keep agreeing to do this,' she said, shaking her head.

His mum's friend was due to pick up the cake at 5 p.m., and they had been working at it nonstop since nine. James had the idea of using caramel to depict electricity coming out of Pikachu's head, but this was proving incredibly difficult to get right.

'Maybe we should give up on the caramel, James – if we want to finish before midnight?'

'Don't be ridiculous, Sara. I'm not going to make a substandard cake. The caramel is essential!'

Eventually, after a lot of work and, to be honest, a little patch of shouting, the cake was finished. They had to admit it looked amazing. And they had managed to finish it at 4.58 p.m. They sat down for two minutes, and at exactly 5 p.m. the doorbell rang.

'I think you should get it, as you were in charge of the cake,' said James's mum.

James opened the door, managing to trip over Graham in the process yet again. He found himself in the arms of the person waiting on the other side, who he realized with a start was Brukka.

'How you doing, little man?' said Brukka, laughing. 'Is this how you usually say hello?'

'Brukka!' squeaked James. 'What are you doing here?'

'I've come to pick up my birthday cake! You know I love Pikachu, right?'

'I can't believe you're here!'

'Me neither, bro. Is it OK if I put you down now?'

James clambered out of Brukka's arms and invited him inside, telling him to watch out for Graham. He couldn't believe what was happening. Brukka was in his house!

Brukka seemed quite taken with Graham and asked if he could pick him up.

'Er, sure, but the last time Mum did that she slipped a disc, so be careful,' James said.

Brukka struggled for a bit and then decided he was going to do himself an injury.

When they were all sitting round the kitchen table with a cup of tea and a big slice of delicious Pikachu cake, Brukka explained the situation.

'When I heard the way DP was talking about you, I didn't like it,' he said. 'Then he told me he was asking you to miss school? No way, man! I had to get rid of him.

'I know what it's like to have a dad who's not there for you,' Brukka said. 'And I felt like DP was trying to force me to do what the record label wanted. So I started thinking, do I know anyone else who's responsible for creating a great rapper? And then I realized, yes, I do.'

'Which great rapper are you talking about?' James asked.

'Oh my God, James, he's obviously talking about you and your mum!' Sara said, rolling her eyes.

Brukka turned to James's mum. 'Mrs Perera, I can't think of anyone better than a mum like you to be my manager. Would you be interested?'

'But . . . I don't know anything about the music industry!' James's mum exclaimed.

'You've got a good heart, and you won't lie to me. That's all I need.'

And, with that, James's mum became Brukka's new manager.

After an hour or so, Brukka said he had to go to a party, so James wrapped up the rest of the cake, and they said their goodbyes.

'So listen, James,' he said at the door, cake balanced in his hands. 'I'll give you a shout in the

Easter holidays to work on some stuff, yeah?'

'That would be amazing,' replied James.

'You're going to need to practise, though, man, because we need to hit the ground running. Oi, lads!!'

Brukka was shouting to some people James couldn't see, but he heard a sound like marching coming from down the hallway. All of a sudden, four guys carrying sound equipment turned up.

'This is a little gift from me, so you can learn your craft, my g. These guys will set it all up for you. By the next time I see you, I want you to be running the sound desk!'

James could not believe it. As Brukka headed off to his party, the men set up the gear and showed James how to get started, and then he and Sara put some tunes on and had a little jamming session.

'OK, maybe I do like rap music after all!' Sara shouted over a particularly loud beat James had created.

These had definitely been the best two days of James's life. He'd stood up to Alfie, he was a real rapper, and he was jamming away with his best friend and his mum. Even Graham seemed to be enjoying the music. Which basically meant his ears were twitching a bit.

'You know what, Sara?'

'What?'

'Today's been another great day, so it might be the right time to try the **DOOM DESSERT** again.'

Sara groaned.

PASS THE MIC!

Think you've got what it takes to impress rap **SUPERSTAR BRUKKA?**
Use this page to start writing raps of your own.
You could write about your favourite things – **THE MORE THE BETTER!**
Here are some prompts to start you off:

CAKE

PETS

TRAINERS

MILKSHAKES

FILMS

THE ZOO

A GREAT DAY OUT

BOOKS

SPORTS

MUSIC

DID YOU ENJOY READING THIS BOOK?

LISTEN TO THE AUDIO EDITION
READ BY
ROMESH RANGANATHAN!

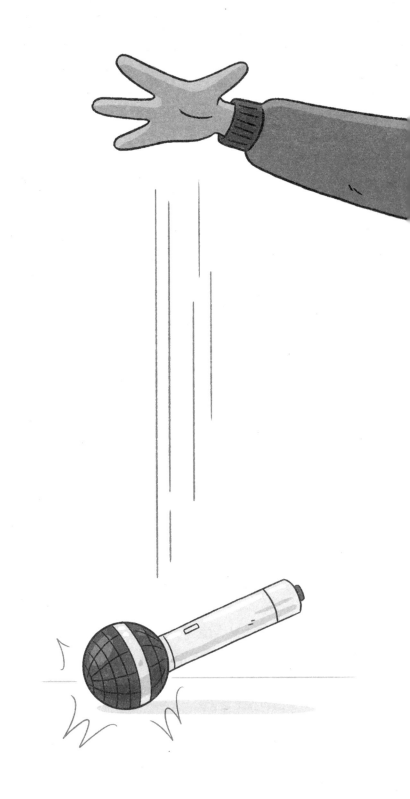